D1740966

Bunker Treasures

A Search For The Amber Room

djv murphy

www.bunkertreasures.com

BUNKER TREASURES

A Search for the Amber Room

Prologue

In the heat of World War II with Germany now occupying most of its neighboring countries, the Führer himself, Adolf Hitler made a mysterious decision.

It was 1942, and after his henchmen had already stolen thousands of artworks, he ordered the theft of another one that was of personal interest to him. This artwork would later become the subject of numerous articles and books and became the focus of treasure hunters around the world.

It is called "The Amber Room."

Originally situated in Pushkin, a small village near St. Petersburg, Russia, The Amber Room was the target of Hitler's seemingly insatiable appetite for all things German.

This one artwork had special meaning to the leader of the Third Reich because centuries before it was made for the Frederick I, the King of Prussia [Germany's predecessor].

After the King's death, his son Fredrick Wilhelm presented it as a gift to Russian Czar Peter The Great. It was to cement the relationship between Prussia and Russia as defenders against the aggression of Sweden.

The gift to the Russian people remained in crates for years until Peter's wife Catherine The Great had it installed in her winter home. Some years later it was packed up and again moved, this time to her summer home in Pushkin.

Over the next hundred seventy plus years, many who had the opportunity to visit the Palace were reportedly awestruck by its beauty. No one had ever seen such opulence on display nor be as captivated by the splendor of The Amber Room.

The Amber Room has been described as a masterpiece of Prussian craftsmanship. Made of thousands of pounds of high-end amber it was bejeweled with hand cut diamonds, rubies, jade, and emeralds. It is considered by many as the most beautiful room ever created.

When the Nazi's invaded Russia in the early 1940's and stole many works of art they also ransacked the former Palace of Catherine The Great.

Word was sent to Hitler about finding The Amber Room, prompting his personal order to seize it and move it to Kaliningrad, Germany. So it was taken apart, put in shipping crates, placed on a train and delivered to the Konigsberg Castle. Ensconced there, it was put on display once again.

Near the end of World War II in the dead of winter with the allies conducting bombing raids in the German countryside as well as targeting German cities, the order went out to move the Amber Room once more.

It again was disassembled, put back in the many crates used to bring it to Kaliningrad, and move it to a safer location.

The Amber Room was never seen again.

Its whereabouts remain a mystery. Some believe that the Russians inadvertently destroyed it when they burned the Konigsberg Castle near the end of the war. The Russians of course deny this version ever happened.

Another theory is that it lies on the bottom of some lake in Germany after the boat carrying it sunk. And some believe that it was buried in some long lost bunker never to be found.

There are still other theories, but the fact remains, The Amber Room is not part of any museum, private collection, or in any government archives. After 1944 it was never to see the light of day ever again.

A last ditch effort to construct bunkers and retrofit existing mines specifically to store the artwork stolen during the war was to no avail. Adolf Hitler committed suicide in April 1945 never to fulfill his dream of creating in Linz, the most important art museum in the world.

His grand theft of The Amber Room and its subsequent moves and whereabouts still remains a mystery after more than 65 years.

However, in the 1990's, the Russian Government recreated a replica of The Amber Room and installed it in the Catherine Palace just outside St. Petersburg.

The story in this book, "Bunker Treasures", is of course fiction, but is based upon actual occurrences and time lines. Perhaps its whereabouts might finally be revealed? Only time will tell.

CONTENTS

Who's Who

The following is an alphabetical list of characters appearing in "Bunker Treasures". Any similarity to real or imagined persons is strictly coincidental. The author apologizes to any and all who might know or actually be one of these characters in real life!

Alderman, Dieter Specialist Interpol Art Theft Task Force, Lyon France

Barlinger, Hans Sole remaining heir to the Barlinger Family Fortune, Linz, Germany.

Bitterman, Manfred Inspector, Interpol Art Theft Task Force; Lyon, France.

Boudreau, Roone Specialist, Interpol Art Theft Task Force, Lyon, France.

Brinlova, Irina Director, Hermitage Museum, St. Petersburg, Russia.

Connelly, Sergeant Joe [also Joe Connelly], World War II American soldier and later major financier and father of Rankin Connelly; New York City.

Connelly, Rankin West Point graduate, fifty year old son of Joe Connelly; art dealer and President of the Connelly Arts Foundation; New York City.

D'Alivia, Mario Collector and dealer in Nazi documents and confidential World War II documents, Salzburg, Austria.

Forsythe, Claude Metropolitan Savannah Police Inspector; Savannah, Georgia.

Goldenson, Charles   United States Senator from New York and Chair Senate Committee on Insurance and Banking, Washington D.C.

Jenkins, Pug   United States Senator from Georgia; member Senate Committee on Insurance and Banking, Washington D.C.

Justov, Yuri   Assistant Director, Russian Ministry of Culture, St. Petersburg, Russia.

Lee, Chuang   Director, Original Reproductions LTD Shanghai, China.

Marshall, Riva   German speaking former art gallery owner; executive assistant to Rankin Connelly at the Connelly Arts Foundation; New York City.

Reinhardt, Klaus   Leader of a German art theft ring, Munich, Germany.

Steinbacker, Horst   Director, Austrian Culture Center, Vienna, Austria.

Vestry III, Robert   Managing Director of the Vestry Law Firm; advisor and legal counsel to Joe Connelly and Rankin Connelly; New York City.

Weinstein, Azure   Partner, Vestry Law Firm; legal counsel to Connelly Arts Foundation, New York City.

Chapter One

Reading of The Will

It seemed so simple at the time.

The plan was to take the map and documents, do some research, and find out exactly what it was that his father kept secret for so many years.

There were of course some unanswered questions such as why his father didn't reveal the mystery begun in the throws of World War II while he was still alive?

Rankin Connelly had experienced a relatively privileged life up to this point as he marked his fiftieth birthday a few months before.

Other than his father's recent sudden death, the most devastating loss during his early years was his mother's death. It didn't seem like thirty years since her passing.

Having no siblings and a father who spent every waking hour running his most successful Wall Street firm, Rankin Connelly was pretty much on his own. That void made him what he was today, a man with a strong take charge character with street smarts and a strong underlying curiosity.

He not only wanted to know who, but also what, when, where, why, and how. It was as if he approached each challenge like he was writing a news story. He covered all the angles.

Of course, being a successful businessman himself, he understood his father's immersion in the world of finances. It was clients with the big bucks, who generously supported the arts. In addition, the art world is where Rankin Connelly made his living.

He figured his father's drive and all consuming interest in the financial markets was his way of filling the emptiness he felt by his wife's untimely death.

His mother and father married much later than most of their contemporaries. Rankin's birth was celebrated by both of them as a miracle of sorts, since his mother was told she would never conceive.

Then just before he was to graduate from West Point, his father shared the bad news about his mother. It was cancer, a cruel and slow killer. The dreaded disease took his mother, and left his father a lonely but determined man.

His father never married again but devoted himself to his career. His energies were directed at making money for his clients and in turn, a fortune for himself.

Now his father was also gone…….a man who lived through World War II…..a decorated combat veteran, and at the age of 77, the victim of a heart attack.

The stress of the financial markets finally did him in, years after he should have retired to enjoy the fruits of his labor.

Rankin never married although his father over the years met many lovely potential mothers of grandchildren he had hoped to spoil.

It wasn't that Connelly was against the idea of marriage. He was a tall, athletic, and very good-looking man and had more than his share of lovelies.

However, no one came along at the specific time that he wanted to tie the knot.

His love life however was never dull, but at times just coincidental to his business life. Socializing to Connelly for just the fun of it had never been on top of his interest list.

He wasn't a country club type, although he shot par and most times could beat the best of his business acquaintances on the links. He concentrated on becoming a successful art dealer and a recognized leader in the art world.

Business success seemed to run in the Connelly family.

Having been a star athlete at West Point and graduating near the top of his class bode well for Connelly. The close-knit fraternity of cadets gave him the kind of contacts that one couldn't buy in the real world.

His military stint after graduation took him to France and Brussels and as a liaison with NATO. He learned languages easily and could speak fluent French and German thanks to his mother's insistence that he study them in boarding school.

There was some talk that he might have had a connection to the Iran-Contra affair, but nothing ever came out of the investigation.

He knew of course some of the players....especially Lieutenant Colonel Oliver North who graduated from West Point's rival the Naval Academy. Rankin being a star running back for Army loved that his team beat Navy in football.

It was in 1986 and Rankin after having been made a Lieutenant first came across the controversial plan to free hostages being held by Iran.

The story involved the clandestine sale of weapons to Iran, in spite of the U.S. arms embargo of them. The kicker was that in addition to the hostage release, that some individuals in the U.S. government would use the money from the arms sale to fund a CIA program in support of Nicaraguan Contras.

The plan was right out of a Hollywood movie script. Get Israel to ship weapons to Iran; then the U.S. would re-supply Israel after getting the cash payment from them; Iran would get the Islamist group Hezbollah to release the six hostages; the cash would go to the insurgents in Nicaragua to overthrow the Sandista Government.

Rankin was not involved, but knew that the whole thing was an idea fraught with danger and political disaster for the Reagan Administration.

He was not one to divulge secrets or pass along hearsay. He learned well from his father that facts were the basis for decision-making.

He made a lot of contacts while in the service through a network of former teammates, classmates, and fellow officers in NATO.

Some of his key art collectors were West Point graduates now leaders of companies, which spent some of their corporate dollars on his suggested art investments.

After the death of this father, and shortly after the memorial service, which was held some weeks later, Connelly was beckoned to the New York Law firm that had handled the legal affairs of his father.

The details of the estate now had been put in order, and the reading of the will was to take place.

Robert Vestry III had been a life long acquaintance of his father. Both traced their relationship back to college days after the war.

Vestry rose through the attorney ranks to head a boutique law firm whose clients included a select group of high finance types. It also didn't hurt that he had a well-honed interest in fine art.

His firm was small as compared to other New York law firms, but was very successful never the less. Rankin used the firm on occasion, but his art business dealings didn't require a lot of outside legal counsel.

After arriving at the plush law offices located in one of the Big Apples all glass high-rise buildings, Connelly was ushered into Vestry's office.

"Welcome Rankin, come in and make yourself comfortable" Vestry said. "I haven't seen you since the memorial service, but want to tell you what a celebration it was of your father's life. You made the most of a solemn occasion and all those in attendance were most impressed by your heartfelt remarks." Vestry noted.

Vestry went on to say that even though Rankin's father was a few years older then himself, they both went back a long way...to their college days after the war.

"He was an amazing man, one of the most successful financiers I've ever known," Vestry commented.

"And as I believe you are aware, his love of the arts resulted in his desire that all of his assets be placed in a foundation to help further his interest," he added.

Connelly replied that yes, his father told him sometime ago that his estate would help create a foundation and he wouldn't be leaving him anything of substance.

"Guess he figured I was already well established in the fine art business and was doing well financially on my own," Rankin said.

Vestry then told Connelly how proud his father was of him and especially his service to the country after graduating from West Point.

"Your father was most aware of the accomplishments in your career and it was his last wish that you head the arts foundation which his estate is creating," he added.

"I have made arrangements therefore that all of his assets will be used to fund this new Connelly Arts Foundation," Vestry said.

He then went on to remark that they both knew his father was a very private man.

"In spite of being such a well known public figure he kept his thoughts and emotions very close to his vest. For example, he never talked much about his service in World War II until just before his death," Vestry added.

Rankin told Vestry that he knew very little about his father's World War II service and that they spoke infrequently about either's military involvement.

Vestry then shared with him information about his father that no one had ever known the details in the years his father was alive. The full story went untold for more than fifty years.

He handed Rankin a well-worn and tattered envelope. Connelly studied the outside, which read "Not to be opened until after my death, and only by my son, Rankin Connelly" and signed by his father, Joseph Connelly.

He then carefully opened the envelope and to his amazement found another envelope. The second envelope had tattered edges and contained a map yellow with age and written in German with a swastika imprint. Plus there were torn pages out of what appeared to be a diary in his father's handwriting, and an inventory list of some sort like a bill of lading written in German.

After examining the envelopes contents Rankin exclaimed, "What the hell..........a map and some papers in German no less and these torn pages in English. And oh, a scribbled note on the top of the envelope."

The note read: Make sure this gets to the 103rd Infantry Headquarters, signed by Sergeant Connelly.

He continued "and what's this,"….. holding up the torn pages written by hand.

Vestry then commented that obviously the request to get the map to the 103rd was never carried out and it was probably the only order his father gave during the war that wasn't met.

He did say however that the reason why the envelope and contents never made it to army headquarters had to do with his father being severely wounded. Afterward he was taken to a hospital in Austria. Within weeks he was shipped back home as the war ended and after his recovery, he was discharged.

Rankin acknowledged that he knew his father had been wounded but never talked much about it.

He also said receiving the map now after his father's death was just unbelievable, but hopefully the accompanying written notes would shed some light on why his father never revealed their meaning during his lifetime.

Then with his interest spiked, he asked Vestry if he knew how his father came to possess the map and other documents.

Thus began a wartime story that added to the mystery of why his father never talked about the map. Now upon his death, he left it to his son as the only tangible thing from his early life.

Vestry said that he first learned of his father's wartime experiences after both had more than a few beers. It was following a grueling episode of college class finals when Joe Connelly was in his twenties, and Vestry in his late teens. They were having a disagreement on America's involvement in the war, and why it took so long to get rid of Hitler.

He then told Rankin the following story as much as he could remember from years ago.

Your father had just been made a Sergeant and was leading a platoon of soldiers, which had broken off from the 103rd Infantry. They were advancing slowly as they pushed the Nazi's back into Germany from France.

It was March 1945, and the objective was to get to Innsbruck to do a mopping up operation while the war was winding down. Hitler wasn't expected to hold out much longer. The Russians were advancing on Berlin, Eisenhower was in a holding pattern in western Germany while Patton was fighting a last Nazi stand in the Ardennes.

Joe Connelly was one of the first soldiers that arrived with his platoon at the scene of a Nazi train derailment...caused by the allies shelling of the area.

He had surmised that the Nazi train had stopped somewhere along the tracks……perhaps to check on its cargo of weaponry and supplies.

Joe had pieced together what he thought had happened before he arrived on the scene of the explosion. His platoon had stopped in the fringes of the woods just at the edge of the clearing. Heavy shelling of the area had just taken place and they were waiting for it to stop. After a short pause in the shelling, he thought he heard noises and voices in the distance, but couldn't see anything in the darkness.

It was almost dawn, with a light snow falling as a steam locomotive came to a halt near a rail siding on the outskirts of Mitterwald, Austria. German voices could be heard in the darkness, with one in particular shouting to unload the train. Over the din of the idling steam engine, the Nazi commander continued his exhortations to his men to move faster in unloading the train.

In the distance, just over the horizon, flashes of light could now be seen. The commander knew what was coming…..the light flashes must be connected to exploding mortar shells. It was too early in the spring for a freak thunderstorm, especially in this hilly area near the German and Austrian border.

As the light from the early dawn illuminated the area, the train's other cars could be seen, and they were laden with weaponry. Only the first few cars behind the engine were being unloaded, with the flatbed cars completing the rest of the train's cargo.

Suddenly, a mortar shell exploded some distance from the train…..but the sound was simultaneous with the flash of light. The mortar was much to close for comfort for the Nazi commander, who again shouted to quickly finish unloading the train.

Now the sunlight was peaking over the edge of the forest that lined the area to the east of the train tracks. A Nazi soldier came to the commander indicating that the last of the crates had been unloaded.

The outline of three civilian men dressed in peasant clothes could now be seen near the entrance of the barn. The Nazi commander approached them as the train's engine began to increase its power in advance for pulling out of the train siding.

All of a sudden, the Nazi commander pulled his luger pistol and shot each of the civilians in the head. As they fell to the ground, he motioned to a few soldiers standing near the train to pick up the motionless bodies and throw them away from the barn and tracks.

As they did, the train began to slowly pull out of the area, as all the soldiers and the commander ran along side and jumped on the moving train.

Then mortar shells fell much closer to the area with the immediate loud explosions being heard. The train had gotten less than a kilometer away from its start when a mortar hit the backside of one of the flatbed cars. Immediately more explosions erupted from the weapons being carried as freight on the flatbed cars.

These explosions caused a chain reaction of other weapons and ammunitions to also explode and suddenly the force of the impact caused the train to lurch back and forth and then derail.

Nazi soldiers bodies were strewn about, covering the white snow crimson red from their bloodied and dismembered limbs. The dead soldiers lay next to the twisted metal of the train's cars and freight.

The explosions ended as abruptly as they had started, but the smoldering metal gave off a red pulsating glow. Only the train's engine could be heard in the otherwise silent morning, slowly puffing out what sounded like the last gasps of a dying beast.

Vestry then continued the story of how Joe Connelly came to possess the Nazi map.

Because your father was one of the first on the scene he saw the dismembered bodies of the Nazi soldiers....of course he had seen plenty of shocking scenes in his service as an infantryman, but none compared to this situation.

He surmised that the train contained the now blown up weaponry to defend Innsbruck for one last stand by the Nazis.

He said that one of his men had come upon the Nazi Commander and called out to his father to come look at something important. The Private had some papers in his hand, which had fallen out of leather pouch lying next to the German soldier. Connelly took them, and seeing that they contained a map, put them back in an envelope and wrote on the outside the inscription which Rankin had just read.

That is until he heard the Nazi commander who was barely alive, speaking over and over, "Sie mussen die kunstarbeit, sie sparen mussen die kunstarbeit sparen".

Then the Nazi passed out and your father thought he was dead.

He stuffed this envelope under his jacket and then as he was walking away, he felt a burning sensation in his shoulder…….he turned around and saw the Nazi commander up on one elbow with his Lugar posed to shoot again, when your father shot a volley of bullets in his direction, killing him instantly.

That was the last your father remembered until he woke up in the army hospital. By then the documents had disappeared and didn't surface again until he was shipped home. Later he found the envelope packed in with his personal belongings.

In the meanwhile, Hitler had committed suicide in his Berlin bunker, and the war ended shortly afterwards.

The documents at that point were meaningless since the war had ended. Your father just put them away in a safe deposit box where they sat for more than 50 years, until just a few weeks ago after his death.

Vestry added, "Your father felt they might be important for you to have, since he inscribed, 'not to be opened until after my death', and they were obviously intended for you to do with as you see fit."

"Now you know the story, but let me caution you…..if you are curious as to where the map might lead…..don't forget that your father never wanted to find out during his lifetime. The whole thing could lead to a dangerous mission or just a wild goose chase," Vestry cautioned.

Rankin responded by saying, "My guess is that he just wanted to put this part of his life behind him and thus kept the documents sequestered away for all these years."

In response, Vestry told Rankin that both he and his associate, Azure Weinstein would be there for him anytime he needed assistance.

At that point Vestry told Rankin that he wanted to introduce his associate who would be available as a special advisor to him in getting the Foundation off and running. He then rang his secretary and asked to have Ms. Weinstein come into his office.

Soon after she arrived Vestry introduced Azure Weinstein to Rankin.

She was much better looking than all of the attorneys he had known, thinking her name Azure certainly matched her beautiful eyes.

Weinstein then offered to assist Rankin in anyway she could, including with the foundation start up.

Rankin thanked her and turned back to Vestry and said he could use all the help offered plus probably a lot more in the weeks and months ahead.

"Don't hesitate to call on either of us directly," Vestry concluded.

Rankin then left the office with a new title as president of a yet to be formed foundation, along with a tattered envelope, and a curiosity about where it all would lead.

He thought about what may come next and was excited about the prospects.

He also had no idea how his life would be turned upside down and the danger he would face in the months to come.

Chapter Two

Unraveling The Mystery

Wasting no time, Connelly found an ideal space in the new developing area of Manhattan formerly called the "meat packing district". Many art galleries and dealers had opened in the past few years and Connelly thought this would be an area where the Foundation could find staff and begin its operations.

After a referral from Vestry's office he agreed to interview a woman named Riva Marshall who Vestry thought might be helpful to Connelly in the Foundation start up.

Marshall was a friend of one of Vestry's German business clients and had extensive experience in fine art.

Connelly invited her to meet at the new offices of the Foundation. He was expecting someone matronly but was surprised that Marshall turned out to be a tall, very attractive, well-dressed, late thirties woman who spoke with a slight German accent.

After introductions, he remarked that in reading her resume' he was surprised not only by her knowledge about the art world but with her ability to speak a number of languages as well.

She noted that her parents had lived in both Austria and Germany while she was growing up and was exposed to a number of languages in school. She also said that her art knowledge came from being an art gallery owner for ten years.

Her grandparents were killed before the war and her mother was placed with another family as a child outside of Linz, Austria. During her early life she lived in a small village in Germany on the Austrian Border and then her parents moved to Bautzen in the Saxony area of Germany.

Connelly explained the reason for the interview by saying that although she had excellent references as noted by the Vestry Law Firm, he wanted to make sure she was the right fit for the Foundation.

He said he was looking for a seasoned grants maker, and in reading her background thought that running her own art gallery might make her valuable as a generalist.

But with her German/Austrian connections he thought she might be of particular help to him in unraveling the mysteries of the map.

He told her that perhaps she would be better suited for a different position than grants maker.

She seemed confused with his comment and asked about the grants position.

"Well you see Ms. Marshall, I want to offer you a different position....to be more of a generalist...kind of a point person for the Foundation," he explained.

Marshall at that point became puzzled and a seemed a bit confused asking what specifically that would entail.

"I know this will sound strange" Connelly said, "but I can't just yet tell you what you would be doing....it would involve some traveling......and a bit of detective work on your part."

Marshall in a somewhat sarcastic tone said "Wait...you are offering me a position but can't tell me what my duties would be....but want me to be a traveling detective?"

Connelly laughed and said he liked her sense of humor and knew it sounded a bit crazy.

She offered that she might better be placed in an executive assistant position then she could help in scheduling and perhaps overseeing the grants area as well.

Connelly said that might work out but he also wondered if as his executive assistant could she be free to travel…..thinking she could be a big help to his unraveling the mysterious documents left by his father.

"Well, the position sounds intriguing, but really Mr. Connelly my love is specifically the arts and in grant making, and that is why I came to see you. As you can see from my resume' I owned art galleries both here in New York and in Germany," she responded.

He said he understood her experience but told her she would not be disappointed if she accepted his offer.

He commented that the pay would be excellent, she could be a big help to him, and as he paused and looked at her in a serious way, "please call me Rankin as my father was the 'Mr. Connelly' in our family."

After a long pause Marshall said, "Mister...I mean Rankin, I would love to help you...but I have other considerations. Let me think about it, and I will get back to you soon."

He then said he understood her need to think about the position, but offered to discuss all the details over dinner that evening.

Somewhat taken aback, Marshall said the dinner invitation was a bit unexpected but would see what she could do about rearranging her schedule.

"Don't worry about it," Connelly said. "I'll have a driver pick you up at eight thirty and I'll meet you at the restaurant".

He had been drawn to various women before this, but somehow he was most intrigued by Ms. Marshall and had felt an immediate connection with her. He thought this could be trouble......or it could be very interesting.

Starting the Connelly Arts Foundation was his longer-term primary interest, but his curiosity about the map's origin was paramount on his mind.

The map was written in German and the area appeared to be based in the vicinity of the German-Austrian border. Even though he could read the language, he believed Ms. Marshall's background would be perfect for helping unravel the mysterious map and documents. And she was so easy to look at as well.

That evening at dinner he explained about how the Foundation concept came about and also as much as he knew about the map and documents left by his father. He filled her in on the background of his father's wartime service and how he came to possess the map and German documents.

He told her that she could be a great help to him in trying to figure out the mystery behind the information left to him by his father.

He was especially excited that she understood German and was familiar with the geography of Germany and Austria having lived there for her childhood and young adulthood.

He got right to the point during dinner and asked if she would help determine what the map meant and where it might lead.

Marshall enthusiastically agreed to help after she found out that she would be going back near her childhood home...after years of living in the U.S.

Something else clicked in that dinner meeting....something Connelly hadn't felt in quite a few years...an instant interest in finding out all he could about Ms. Marshall as a woman.

After a few weeks following her agreement to become his executive assistant, he gathered a number of documents pertaining to the end of the war. His West Point contacts were continuing to pay dividends.

He wanted to know more about the initials on the map and if indeed Hitler had authorized it personally as he had hoped.

He also read about Hitler's well-documented obsession with building the world's greatest Art Museum in Linz, Austria.

Using the Foundation's conference room, Connelly covered a blackboard and a corkboard with the documents found in his father's tattered envelope. Displayed was a large version of a map of the German/Austrian border near a village named Mitterwald.

On her first day as his executive assistant, Marshall was ushered into the conference room by the receptionist and was greeted by Connelly formally as Ms. Marshall.

As the receptionist closed the conference room door Marshall said "Hello 'Mister' Connelly [pausing and then smiling flirtatiously].......if we are going to work together, let's drop the formalities, please call me by my first name, like you did a few weeks ago after our dinner"!

"OK....OK. Please have a seat," Connelly said laughingly. "Now as I was about to say....before we get down to business....I have to ask you to keep everything we discuss here today in complete secrecy. We are embarking on a trip through uncharted territory....it could be dangerous and lead to an unwanted destiny.... as my father's attorney warned."

Marshall pledged her confidentiality and in looking around the room noted all the effort he had put into the preparation for this first session.

Connell then highlighted each document and gave an overview of his interpretation. Speaking about the map he said it appeared to contain information about a shipment of either weapons or some type of contraband and its hiding place.

Marshall reviewed the original and indicated that the seal on the map was an official Nazi stamp from the Fuhrer's office and contained Hitler's' initials. She noted it could have also been signed by Martin Bormann, Hitler's' right hand man.

She showed Connelly the notation "Highly Confidential" and the Nazi pressed seal.

"This was only used by someone in Hitler's inner circle," Marshall pointed out. "I have no doubt about its' origins but I can't quite make out the maps termination point.

Connelly interrupting said, "So you're sure about the maps authenticity?"

"Rankin.....I am fairly certain about the map.....but I think you might already be in the field looking for the answers to what the map is suggesting?" Marshall responded.

Connelly laughingly said, "OK, I am just very anxious to find out where this leads, as it is the last connection to my father."

Marshall said she understood but wanted to explore the hand written notations and study his fathers torn pages from the diary. Of special interest was the listing of what appeared to be a mixture of code names for weapons and other materials all in German, organized and typed cleanly.

After spending time looking at the documents which Connelly had laid out and the large replica map, Marshall said she believed one notation on the map said "Top Secret: For the Commandant's eyes only, dated March, 1945 and refers to Linz."

"Linz as in the museum Hitler was going to have his architect Albert Speer build for him in Austria?" Connelly asked.

Marshall said his assumption could be right because it was known that Hitler had made a significant effort in planning for the proposed museum.

Connelly's research also indicated that Hitler had catalogs made as the art inventory grew for his proposed museum in Linz.

"Damn this is getting very interesting," Connelly said. "I know Hitler and one of his closest aides Martin Bormann had buried gold, artwork, and lots of cash at Altausse and other salt mines in Austria...if and when they had to leave their headquarters bunker in Berlin."

Marshall then offered an opinion that the map might indicate the location of a bunker since the Germans were using them to store or hide a lot of things.

She then pointed out a specific part of the map to Connelly where she identified the often used Nazi symbol for a bunker.

The symbol was located in what appeared to be a cluster of small buildings near a railroad track.

Connelly was now getting very interested in every detail of the map. He told Marshall he thought she was right and asked to look at the more expanded version of map. This blown up version was posted on the wall, and showed small boxes near the train tracks.

Marshall said her guess was that these boxes represented a cluster of buildings representative of a small farm or collective, adjacent to railroad tracks.

They were making a lot more headway than he first expected and sooner than not, would want to move ahead with a visit to the spot where the map lead.

So shortly after this initial meeting at the Foundation's offices, Marshall joined Connelly in planning an exploratory trip to Germany.

She offered to contact one of her former associates, an attorney in Germany, to first scope out the area. Connelly was at first wary of this plan, as he didn't want anyone to become suspicious of their search for what the map represented.

She said she would only tell the German attorney, what she believed was the type of property noted on the map. She knew he was familiar with the area outside of the village she identified by her research.

There would be no mention of the map or the reason for the inquiry only that she was working with a friend who expressed an interest in buying property in that area.

During the next few months Connelly continued the organization effort of the Connelly Art Foundation, now referred to as the CAF. Staff was hired, including a chief operating officer, who would manage the internal affairs of the Foundation.

This freed up Connelly from dealing with the administrative details of the Foundation, and allowed him to concentrate on unraveling the mystery of the Nazi map and accompanying documents.

After this interim period, the German attorney contacted Marshall and said he thought he had found the place she had asked about.

It was an abandoned property and no one had lived there since WWII, and was in an area, which had been tied up in an estate for years. The only known owners had disappeared near the end of the war.

The attorney also noted that the local village government was happy to have someone interested in it.

Connelly jumped at the chance to buy it sight unseen, and was happy that in mid-2009 that the Dollar was still holding its own against the Euro.

Connelly knew whatever the price he would get a good deal. But first things first he would personally inspect the property location. He didn't want to raise any suspicions about his intentions.

It also helped that Marshall had heard of the nearby village from her parents as a child. It was on the same train line, which was used during the War by the Nazi's to send people to the concentration camp at Ebensee, Austria.

It made sense then to both Connelly and Marshall that this fit the description of the map's location...on a train line...an abandoned farm...with buildings right near the train tracks.

Now it all seemed to be coming together. So shortly after getting confirmation from Riva's German Attorney about the information on the property, they set off for Germany and Austria.

Things were moving very fast for Connelly. First the discovery of the map after his father's death, then organizing the Foundation, finding someone to assist him in the search and developing a possible relationship with her, and now the exploration of the possible site illustrated by the mysterious map.

Chapter Three

The Plot Thickens

After landing at the Munich Airport in Germany, Connelly and Marshall rented a Land Rover and headed out toward the Austrian-German Border. The road is hilly and winding and traverses through the countryside not far from where Hitler lived near Berchtesgaden some 65 years before.

After driving for what felt like hours on narrow and winding roads they came into a small village in the area thought to be near where the farm might be located.

As they entered the small village, Marshall sees some men sitting outside a bar and asks Connelly to stop so she can ask directions.

The car pulls in front of the bar and she gets out of the car, approaches the men and speaks to them as Connelly watches from the car.

After a few minutes one of the men points down a road as the other men appear to be laughing.

Riva then gets back in the car and she tells Rankin to proceed in the direction pointed out by the man.

Wondering why the men laughed, he asked if she said something funny to the men.

She said that it wasn't anything she said, but they started laughing when one of the men said ghosts haunted the place they were looking for.

Riva said that although these men were born after the war they did say that no one had lived in this particular property as long as they could remember.

After about six kilometers, Connelly saw a narrow paved road crossing over a set of railroad tracks which turns into a narrow one lane dirt road that is overgrown with weeds adjacent to the tracks.

He stops the car after driving to a spot adjacent to the tracks and near some out buildings.

They then get out of the car and begin walking around the unkempt property. They see various small buildings and a larger one near the tracks where the fences are partially broken.

Riva after looking around at the desolate sight of weathered buildings and overgrown landscape, comments that she feels this could be the place.

She tells Rankin that if no one has lived here since the war it could mean one of two things, whatever might have been put in the bunker is long gone, or no one ever found the bunker's location. She added that it wasn't going to be as easy as they first thought.

He then suggests that they check the main house, get settled for the night, and begin the search of the out buildings bright and early the next morning.

Marshall's German attorney, in anticipation that Connelly might purchase the property, received permission from the local village official to have the main house cleaned and set up for a possible short stay.

Rankin noticed that although the main house looked run down from the outside, it had been very helpful of the attorney to get the inside set up so well for their stay.

Riva said that she had asked him to have it cleaned and stocked with food, just in case they decided to stay a few days.

Rankin thought to himself that he hoped the attorney only entered the farmhouse and didn't look around anywhere else while he was there.

After getting settled in and as the sun began to set in the west over the ridge of trees at the edge of the overgrown pasture, they had dinner and shared a bottle of wine.

Both were tired and Rankin began to yawn as the long day was catching up with him.

Seeing that he was tired, Riva got up from the dinner table and began to rub his neck and massage his shoulders.

She remarked "Oh you poor dear.....let me give you a neck massage."

He couldn't help remarking to Riva about her extra special talents, which weren't listed in her resume'.

Riva responded in a very sexy voice, which he hadn't heard from her before.

"Rankin you always know what to say to a woman at just the right time", she whispered in his ear. "Come with me to the bedroom, I want to show you another talent that you didn't read on my resume'!"

She walks with him into the dimly lit bedroom, pulls the shades closed, and walks by herself into the bathroom and turns on the shower. In a minute she calls out and beckons him to join her.

She was standing naked with the shower door open as Rankin walked in the bathroom and quickly undressed. The sight of her lithe athletic body with full firm breasts stopped him in his tracks. He couldn't help starring at her standing there looking so sensual.

He hadn't shared a shower with a woman in a long time, but the soft flow of the water and the feel of her body against his began to reinvigorate him.

Riva took the soap and slowly lathered his upper body turning him around so that she stood behind him. With her arms around him, pressing her full breasts against his back she moved the soap gently down his abdomen and caressed his now erect manhood with her fully lathered hands.

Connelly wanted to take her then, but after turning around and kissing her deeply, he cleansed both of them and dried her taught body with the towels laid out on the vanity.

The couple then made their way to the bed and began kissing passionately. Riva slowly began moving her lips from his neck, kissing his muscular chest, down and down as Rankin moaned with pleasure as her mouth enveloped him.

All of a sudden gunshots rang out from an area outside the house interrupting their most sensual moments.

Connelly jumped out of bed and quickly moved toward the slightly illuminated window and slowly pulled back the blinds.

He cautioned Riva to move to the floor near the bed and stay there as he pulled his pants on and quickly slipped his feet into the shoes left near the door.

Riva excitedly called out to him not to leave the room in his effort to discover what caused the sound of gunshots coming from the driveway area of the house.

"Don't worry, I won't do anything stupid, but I just can't stay in here and wait it out. I'll be very careful," Rankin said.

He then walked cautiously to the back door, crouches low as he walks down the few steps to the overgrown back yard area and slipped through the fence opening.

As he quietly approaches the front of the house he hears the roar of a car engine and sees the darkened image hastily drive away from the house. The moon is casting a dim light illuminating the area and he sees the Land Rover and looks at what appears to be deflated tires.

This was not the only thing the sound of the bullets deflated. It just was not the same romantic mood once Rankin went back in the house.

He and Riva then spent the next hour trying to figure out who and why someone would vandalize the car but nothing else.

The next day he got the answer to the questions he posed the previous night.

Under the windshield wiper of the Range Rover was a folded piece of paper. The words were pasted on it from a newspaper and laid out like an old movie ransom note.

The pasted lines contained words in German and were pieced together to spell out a sentence.

Rankin asked Riva what she made of it. After scanning the document, she agreed with him that the German words were "we don't want you here, leave now."

"If these jerk-offs think we are leaving after having come this far, they should know we aren't going to be scared off by punks shooting out our tires and leaving this bullshit threat," he said emphatically.

Riva agreed with his assessment, and so the couple with renewed interest began searching the property, which might lead them to unraveling the map's mysteries.

After looking most of the day, checking under floorboards, around the main house and in the various outbuildings, they began to get the feeling that the "bunker treasures" were just a myth.

Both of them were getting tired and discouraged and thought about giving up the search for whatever was noted on the map. But then they finally located a part of the old barn, which hadn't been disturbed for more than sixty years

One small section of the floor creaked as they stepped on it, while the rest of the floor was as solid as concrete.

Sweeping away the debris and straw, the couple discovered something strange.

They pushed a piece of timber out of the way and then saw a trap door partially dislodged in the floor.

Opening it slowly, Rankin carefully descended the dusty flight of stairs. He entered a large chamber filled with crate after crate, illuminated dimly by his flashlight. Riva followed him stepping gingerly down the dark stair treads.

"Oh my God look at this....it's just incredible. No one would ever have believed it," Rankin exclaimed.

Once Riva steps on the dimly lit floor, he picks her up, dropping his flashlight, and as he twirls her around her flashlight illuminates crate after crate in various sizes laying about the cavernous bunker. Riva laughs with excitement.

After putting her down and kissing her in celebration, Connelly suddenly sees something metallic near the base of the stairs and stoops over to pick it up.

He finds a fully loaded German Luger…..which he assumes must have been dropped in haste as the Nazi soldier left the bunker.

Marshall remarks that she hoped it was the only weapon left behind when the crates were being stored in the bunker some sixty plus years ago

Connelly jokes, "Maybe it will come in handy later!"

"God, I certainly hope not," Riva responds.

They kiss again as their flashlights fall to the floor giving an eerie cast to the cavernous bunker. The search for the illusive treasures hidden by the Nazis for so many years had ended in success.

In an effort to see as much as possible during this visit, they decided to buy special temporary lighting. So they left the farmhouse and drove past the closest village to a larger town some distance away. They wanted to avoid raising any suspicion in Mitterwald about their activities.

The lighting came in handy after the discovery of so many crates in the main bunker. Rankin even found a tunnel passageway leading to the main house, and another to different room also filled with crates.

Investigating the passages while Riva began to open the crates with tools brought with them, Rankin noticed a leather pouch, stooped down and picked it up.

Opening it, he found documents written both in German and Russian and another map, which was soiled and almost unreadable.

Later research showed that the documents found in the pouch, referred to The Amber Room.

Their quest for information pertaining to the Nazi map had been fulfilled. Now a new challenge faced them having to do with the long lost Amber room.

This discovery was not only to provide a strengthening of their romantic entanglement but the beginning of a path fraught with danger.

Chapter Four

The Interrogation

A year had passed since Connelly quickly developed the arts foundation into one of the leading private funders of the arts in the country. He had become somewhat of a celebrity in the art world, even though his earlier career was spent wheeling and dealing with other major players.

But as the saying goes *'that was then, and this is now.'*

Looking back on what had transpired, Rankin was surprised and more than delighted that in addition to finding the hidden bunker, that there was also another connection with his deceased father.

Early on he had hoped there was a link between his father finding the mysterious map and the actual location of the bunker.

At times however, he thought perhaps it might have been better to wait longer to carryout the search. Did he rush to quickly into the trying to find out what his father ignored for all those years?

But what happened after the bunker treasures discovery turned out to be the real adventure. A journey that would prove challenging to his reputation and a destination that would leave him so emotionally wounded.

The warning by his father's attorney Vestry had come true, at least the part relating to the search leading to a dangerous mission.

His travels took him to many places in Europe including St. Petersburg in an effort to gain Russian acceptance of the fact that they held many stolen artworks from World War II. His interest in this historical connection expanded the mission of the Foundation to include finding the rightful heirs to a trove of art stolen during the war.

Following the Foundation's inaugural year and being recognized for many of the Foundation's creative grants, Rankin was a sought after speaker in the art world. He declined most invitations because of his continued interest in the results of solving the mystery behind the old map.

However, one invitation was most graciously accepted. This particular organization was the recipient of the first significant grant from the Foundation.

Rankin had personally sought out an institution, which was the leader in arts education. One whose mission was to not only educate but to do so with a practical outcome. Preparing its students for careers in the creative arts field was a key ingredient of success in his mind.

After catching an early flight from Newark Airport just outside New York City, he arrived in Savannah where he was to give the commencement speech at the Southern Institute of Art and Design [SIAD]. The institution was the recipient of the Foundations first major grant.

Upon arriving in Savannah, Rankin and Riva checked into one of the downtown boutique hotels overlooking the Savannah River. He asked her to make a field visit to the historic Telfair Museum while he tended to his commencement speech.

Later that morning he went to the theatre where the S.I.A.D. commencement took place. A banner reading "Welcome Rankin Connelly.....C.A.F." was draped on the theatre curtain behind Connelly as he addressed the assembly. The theatre was filled to capacity with graduates, families, friends and faculty.

He used the occasion to remind the graduates of the global impact of the arts. Reflecting back on history he told them how nations have used art as the bounty taken from those they conquered.

He said that throughout history "it's an unfortunate result of wars that art treasures are stolen, sometimes destroyed, leaving a void in the cultures of the conquered nations....and humanity the poorer for it."

He then told the personal story of his father's experience as it was getting near the end of World War II. He said the Allies including his father and many more brave American soldiers, were pushing back the Nazis through France, Austria into the heart of Germany.

Hitler in his Berlin headquarters was preparing for the worst.

The Nazi plan for the possible outcome of the war, was building underground bunkers. In some of those bunkers went the booty Hitler's regime stole from overrun countries and countless individuals.

He noted that history books report the end came quickly for Hitler's reign of terror in late April 1945.

And now more than 65 years later the trove of his stolen treasures is still being discovered.

Rankin said his own experience led him to learn first hand what Hitler had himself directed to be hidden in a bunker.

He told the S.I.A.D. audience that he had made a discovery of perhaps historical significance regarding the long lost Amber Room. He cautioned however that only time would tell if it turns out that way.

And with tongue in cheek he remarked that someday he might write a book about his experiences of the past year.

Departing from his more serious prepared remarks about wars and stolen art work, Rankin told the group about a much more happier subject

He remarked that S.I.A.D was recognized as the leading art and design school in the world something everyone in the room already knew and believed.

He then offered his congratulations to those in attendance at the Southern Institute of Art and Design graduation ceremonies.

After those complementary remarks, Connelly was interrupted as the audience began to vigorously applaud.

"Please, please, I appreciate your applause... but let me finish by saying it is my privilege on behalf of the Foundation to present a full scholarship to be awarded annually to an aspiring art and design major.....to be selected by a committee of students and faculty", he said.

Rankin then received a standing ovation from the audience who continued to cheer as he departed the stage.

As he walked across toward the backstage of the theatre he noticed two uniformed police officers and a mid forties rumpled looking plain-clothes policeman.

The police in turn watch as he walks toward them with the applause continuing and then they approach him.

The plain-clothes policeman greets him by identifying himself.

"Mr. Connelly, very nice presentation, I'm Inspector Forsythe of the Metro Police and these are my associates. We have a few questions for you and ask that you accompany us down to the station."

Thinking they are joking he said, "What? Here I thought you were going to give me a police escort!"

Inspector Forsythe at this point begins to get agitated and indicates to Connelly that they can either walk out like gentlemen or they could put him in handcuffs and give him the "perp walk" as a reference to the New York Police way of escorting suspects.

Reacting with a perplexed look on his face, Rankin shrugs his shoulders and walks with the group through the stage door to an awaiting police car.

After they arrive at the Police station later that morning, Rankin is permitted to make one phone call. He reaches Vestry's Law Firm in New York and tells his personal attorney, Azure Weinstein about the situation. She indicates she will come to Savannah on the next flight that day, and cautions him not to speak to any of the authorities until she arrives.

He knew she would respond quickly, and in many situations during the past year, was a good advisor to him.

He also knew however, that at times she appeared to want to move beyond their professional relationship. He never encouraged that because of his feelings for Riva.

By early evening, Connelly's attorney, Azure Weinstein arrives from New York and joins him in the police station conference room where he is awaiting her arrival.

He is of course is very happy to see her, and said how much he appreciates making this emergency trip to Savannah on such short notice.

Weinstein tells him that she was lucky to catch the last flight from Newark Liberty Airport and offers the opinion that there is no reason for him to be detained by the police.

She indicates as much to Inspector Forsythe strongly suggesting that there is no legal basis for holding Connelly unless charges are filed against him.

Forsythe responds, "Now just wait a minute Ms. Weiner". Ms. Weinstein interrupts and said, "Excuse me, the name is Ms. Weinstein!"

Nodding his head Inspector Forsythe indicates that Connelly is being held so that agents from Interpol could question him. He said that his department was contacted a few months ago and was asked to detain Mr. Connelly if he presented himself in Savannah.

Ms. Weinstein then asked for what purpose would Interpol be interested in questioning him.

Inspector Forsythe responded, "for dealing in stolen artworks".

After spending the better part of the day in the holding pen, Connelly's patience was wearing thin.

"Stolen artwork!" exclaimed Connelly. "How utterly preposterous. Neither you nor Interpol have any basis for this unfucking believable accusation," he yelled.

Weinstein also chimed in and said "Mr. Connelly is absolutely right. This isn't a case of Homeland Security where you can just hold someone without charges. Furthermore he is the head of one of our country's leading arts foundations and a highly respected member of the business community."

In response, Inspector Forsythe said all of that may be true, but under the law of Georgia someone may be kept 48 hours without being charged with a crime. However if Connelly and Weinstein persisted, then charges would be filed for fencing stolen goods worth millions....a felony.

"Let's get real Inspector Forsythe," Ms. Weinstein responded. "You know that suspicion alone isn't a basis for an arrest. Now either charge my client or let him leave immediately."

Inspector Forsythe then said, "I'll tell you what. We'll defer the charges under the condition that Mr. Connelly does not leave the State of Georgia until Interpol arrives.

"Not acceptable" Weinstein replies.

At this point Rankin interrupts and says that he would rather have this cleared up now then to defer it and agrees to stay for a few days until Interpol arrives.

"Then it's a deal?" Inspector Forsythe questions, as Ms. Weinstein let's out a sigh and resigns herself to the agreement.

Both Rankin and Weinstein then answer "deal".

Chapter Five

The Briefing

After the brief interrogation at the Metro Police Headquarters, Connelly and Weinstein head back to his hotel in Savannah.

Once back at the hotel, they go to his suite where his associate Riva Marshall is waiting. After introductions, Rankin explained what had happened during the day.

Riva said how upsetting it was that she couldn't reach him after the graduation ceremony, and said that no one at the Institute knew what had happened.

He explained that he didn't have access to a phone, except to call New York and that the police had taken his cell phone from him.

Rankin then asked her to order room service for the three of them including wine. That would give him time to explain to Ms. Weinstein what had happened to cause Interpol to be so interested in speaking with him.

He then began briefing Ms. Weinstein by telling the story of what happened before her boss Robert Vestry brought her into that first meeting in his office.

Vestry shared some startling information with me. I was surprised to learn during the meeting with Vestry that my father had kept a life long secret.

He said that even though my father was older then him, they went to college together after the war. He told me the story of how my father was wounded near the end of World War II, and about what he wanted me to do after his death.

Vestry tried to explain why he kept this secret so long by saying that even though my father was a public figure, he was also a very private man....played things and emotions very close to his vest.

For example he never talked much about his service in World War II until just before his death.

Vestry also said my father was an amazing man, one of the most successful financiers that he had ever known. His love of the arts resulted in his desire that all of his assets be placed in a foundation to help further his interest.

I knew he wanted his interest in the arts to continue even after his death. He had told me that his estate would help create a foundation and he wouldn't be leaving anything of substance to me. Guess he figured I was already well established in the fine art business.

It was his last wish that I head up the arts foundation, which his estate created.

But Vestry also shared one other thing with me. He said my father had kept something he found in the war for all these years and gave me a tattered manila envelope. Before I opened it I read the inscription on the outside. "This is to be opened only upon my death, Joseph R. Connelly."

When I opened the sealed envelope I found three things....a map, some documents in German, and what appeared to be torn pages from a diary my father had kept during the war.

The map was in German and the envelope containing it had a scribbled note on the top. 'Make sure this gets to the 103rd Infantry Headquarters, signed Sergeant Joe Connelly'. Obviously his order was never carried out.

But I found out that he wasn't in a position to give the map to anyone, as he was wounded right after he found it. He was taken to a hospital in Austria...then he was shipped back home. In a few weeks the war ended and he was discharged after his recovery.

Vestry also shared the story with me about how he was wounded.

He said my father told him about it, after sharing a few beers during his college days. My father was one of the first soldiers to arrive on the scene of a Nazi train derailment...caused by the allies shelling of the area.

It was near the border of Germany and Austria. My father led a small platoon of soldiers after having lost both another Sergeant and the Lieutenant in an earlier battle.

After mortars hit the Nazi train, the platoon came upon the scene. He discovered something surprising and important in the wreckage of the train. Vestry said my father painted this word picture.

Smoldering train...Nazi soldiers bodies strewn about, light snow falling, the ground soiled with the blood of the Germans, U.S. Soldiers walking cautiously among the debris.

A few soldiers approach the wreckage when one of them notices a partially opened leather satchel lying next to a German officer's body with documents hanging out of it.

One of the privates in his platoon yells to my father to come look at his discovery.

My father sees a satchel lying on the ground next to the body of the German officer and he pulls out some papers. Thinking they might be of some importance, stuffs the papers into his jacket after jotting a short note down on the envelope which contained a map appearing to have been signed by Hitler.

As he is walking away he feels a sharp pain in his shoulder, which whips his body around, and he spots the German officer with a gun in his hand ready to shoot again, and my father kills him with a volley of shots from his rifle.

"Oh my God, Rankin," Ms. Weinstein interrupts. "I can understand now how this must all be so unsettling for you. Your father's death, the sad story of his being wounded in the war, the shock having his diary and map given to you.....and now this Interpol investigation."

She continued, "No wonder he never wanted to talk about his war experiences.....obviously the map and other documents he left you have taken on a more personal meaning since you know how he came to possess them."

'Well", Connelly responded, "Vestry also said my father wanted me to know that the contents of the envelope could lead to danger or an unwanted destiny...the decision on what I do with them was entirely mine."

At that point Riva Marshall added that in her opinion, it wasn't just the map and the diary, which could have led to danger, but his father knew Rankin's curiosity would lead him to find out what the map and documents meant. It was to be his legacy....more than just heading the Foundation.

Weinstein then asked Connelly what he did after receiving the documents. She was particularly interested in the association of Connelly and Marshall, not knowing her boss had recommended her to Connelly.

Rankin noted that after he began setting up the staffing for the Foundation, he met Ms. Marshall and....

"Wait" Weinstein said, "I lost you somewhere....first you mentioned the reading of the will, then receiving a map, getting named to head the Foundation, and how does meeting Ms. Marshall fit into this?"

Riva then interjected "What he is trying to say is that my involvement is directly related to his receiving the map and documents which were in German. Mr. Vestry thought I would be someone that Rankin could use to help in the early stages of creating the Foundation. It was afterward that I began helping to unravel the mystery behind the map.

Rankin then continued by telling Ms. Weinstein about the initial days of organizing the foundation and that he knew about the need to get the best staff possible.

He said once staff was hired, they needed to secure registrations with state and federal overseers, apply for and secure IRS status for the new 501 [c] 3 organization.

And of course guidelines had to be developed for the submission of grant applications, and the making of grants.

"I was fortunate to hire a chief operating officer to manage all the administrative details." he said.

"At this point we began the unraveling of the map's origin and leading us to the discovery of the bunker." he added.

Weinstein responded by telling Rankin that she didn't understand why Interpol developed such a interest in him at this point.

"I am assuming Interpol's misguided interest is related to what we found in the bunker," Rankin said.

"Do you think you are being set up by someone who might want what you found?" Weinstein asks.

Marshall interjects "What about Justov and the Russians. They definitely have an interest and should be on top of the list."

Weinstein now intrigued by Marshall's comment asks Connelly to tell her about the Russians.

He responds by telling her it's a long story but has to do with information regarding the Amber Room, stolen by the Nazi's during World War II.

One of the documents we found in the bunker was a cryptic note about the Amber Room. I knew about its theft during the war by Hitler and that it had never been located. I also knew the Russian government would love to have any lead on its possible whereabouts. It was this connection that I thought I could use to encourage Russia to join with other countries and return the art stolen during the war years.

Riva and I flew to St. Petersburg to meet with the head of the Hermitage Museum. It has served as a repository for much of the art work taken by the Russian Army from Germany at the end of the war.

We had contacted the museums director Irina Brinlova and indicated we wanted to present a couple of historic paintings to the museum. Our objective was to see if we could convince the Russians to join with other countries in the return of stolen art work to the owners.

We had hoped to meet for dinner but instead a guy by the name of Yuri Justov showed up in her place.

He said he was a deputy director of the Russian Cultural Mission and was there to find out what exactly we were proposing to the government.

I said the Connelly Foundation had started a program to locate art work stolen during the war years and help foster its return to the rightful owners or heirs.

He responded by saying the Russian government was not in possession of any stolen art works and that any art taken from Germany was considered restitution for the damages done by the Nazis.

Knowing that we weren't getting anywhere I asked Mr. Justov if he would pass along a note to Ms. Brinlova. I wrote on my business card "Amber Room Information" and put it in an envelope and handed it to him.

Following the dinner, Mr. Justov asked if we would be interested in going to the theatre to see the famous Restov Ballet which was having their final performance that evening.

Ms. Marshall was most interested in the proposal so we accepted the tickets and later went to the ballet.

Before leaving the restaurant Mr. Justov said he would see if he could set up a meeting with Ms. Brinlova for the following day, and would confirm early in the morning.

Following the theatre we returned to our hotel room to find that it had been ransacked. The art work however was left undisturbed, only our personal items were spread all over the room. Fortunately nothing of substance was missing.

Early the next morning we received a message from the front desk that a meeting had been arranged by Mr. Justov with the museum director. We were to be picked up at 10 a.m. in the hotel lobby and driven to the Hermitage Museum for our appointment with Ms. Brinlova.

At the appointed hour, we were accompanied by Mr. Justov to the Museum where the four of us met. The Museum is housed in a magnificent building with hundreds of artworks on display and thousands more in storage floors below the building.

I said we had enjoyed the Restov Ballet but our hotel room was broken into during our absence. Mr. Justov apologized and said that there had been a rash of recent burglaries in hotels, and the police were working to solve such crimes.

Of course, we both knew this was not a burglary, but a failed attempt at finding out about our Amber Room information.

Our discussion with Ms. Brinlova then centered upon the missing Amber Room and our discovery of a possible lead on its whereabouts. Both she and Justov inquired about our motivation for sharing this information and the Foundation's donation of the artwork.

I told them that the Foundation wanted the Russians to join other countries in agreeing to inventory the stolen artwork and return it to those it was stolen from during the war.

Ms. Brinlova spoke the party line saying that the Russians do not acknowledge any art work was stolen after the war by the Russian Army, nor do they plan to return any artwork in their possession as it rightfully belongs to the Russian people.

Justov was a bit more direct when he accused us of trying to barter with them over a subject which was closed many years ago.

At that point I knew it was a losing proposition to continue the conversation, so I indicated that if their position changed, the Foundation would be in a *position to help them with the return of stolen artwork.*

We left then for the hotel to pick up our luggage and the artwork we had wanted to present to the Hermitage Museum as a way of breaking the ice with them.

At the Pulkovo International Airport outside of St. Petersburg, we encountered more Russian hospitality when we were denied permission to take the artwork out of the country which we brought with us. It seemed as if it was a set up job by Justov but we had no choice but to leave them or miss our flight back to the U.S. We've never heard a word from them since then.

As Connelly ended his story about the Russian visit, Weinstein remarked what an incredible situation they found themselves in and that perhaps Justov or his cronies could be involved somehow.

"But it doesn't add up when you consider they haven't made any contact with you since that meeting last year" Weinstein said.

At that point with the hour getting late and having spent a trying day with the commencement speech and then the police interrogation, Connelly suggested they all take a break until the next morning.

Room service had arrived with dinner so the three of them dined together in the suite, and then parted ways until the next morning.

At breakfast he would conclude the briefing of Ms. Weinstein of his involvement with the map, Foundation, and search for where the map led him.

Chapter Six

Interpol

In Lyon, France at the headquarters of Interpol, the task force, which has been tracking stolen artwork in Europe, is meeting. The building is very imposing but somewhat forbidding in its setting, surrounded by high chain link fences with sharp razor like protrusions.

One of the major programs of Interpol is the protection of cultural artifacts. Their stated purpose from the Interpol website is as follows:

The theft of cultural objects affects developed and developing countries alike. The two countries most affected by this phenomenon are France and Italy. The illicit trade in cultural objects is sustained by the demand from the arts market, the opening of borders, the improvement in transport systems and the political instability of certain countries.

It is difficult to gauge the extent of the trade for two reasons:

- *The theft is very often not discovered until the stolen objects are found on the official arts market.*

- *Countries send very little information to INTERPOL and many do not keep statistics on this type of criminality.*

In order to combat the theft of cultural property, the relevant organizations and the public need to be made more aware of the problem. International organizations must lead the way in this fight, and since 1947, INTERPOL has been specifically involved. The first international notice on stolen works of art was published in that same year. Since then, the *techniques have evolved greatly and INTERPOL has developed a highly efficient system for circulating information in the form of a database accessible to <u>INTERPOL member countries</u>, as well as the more widely available INTERPOL Stolen Works of Art CD-ROM.*

These web pages have been created to further extend the circulation of information concerning stolen works of art, and include: The <u>most recent</u> stolen works of art reported to INTERPOL

- *Works of art recovered by the police during their enquiries and for which <u>owners have not been identified</u>*

- *Works of art recorded in the INTERPOL database and CD-ROM which have been <u>recovered</u>*

- *The latest INTERPOL <u>posters</u> showing the most sought after stolen works of art*

INTERPOL would like to encourage you to make extensive use of its services, and play an active role in the pooling and exchange of information. This is one of the most important contributions you can make to help curb the erosion of our cultural heritage.

At the same time that Connelly, Marshall and Weinstein were meeting, Interpol agents were preparing to come to Savannah and meet with their prime suspect regarding a large European art theft.

Inside Interpol Headquarters are three men gathered in a small conference room. They are discussing a case involving an American and a series of artworks that have been thought to be lost for sixty plus years.

The three Interpol staff stood around a large bulletin board, which is adorned with photocopy pictures of artwork.

The schematic shows diagrams of lines connecting names, dates, and places of various artworks, which have been identified as being stolen.

The lead member of the task force is Inspector Bitterman, medium build, balding, mid fifties and fierce looking. His background includes 25 years as an Interpol agent and the last few years he headed the stolen artwork task force. It has been a trying time for Interpol because of the rise in the trafficking of stolen works especially in Eastern Europe.

The two men with Bitterman include Roone Boudreau; blond tall mid thirties Frenchman, and Chance Alderman; early thirties, medium height Afro-American who is on loan to Interpol from the New York City Police Department.

The inspector is upset and tells the men that he doesn't like what happened in Savannah with the detainment of Rankin Connelly.

"Why couldn't they wait for you two to arrive...before letting the dog out of the bag?" He lamented.

Trying to hold back a laugh, Alderman says, "You mean 'cat out of the bag' inspector.

"Yes, yes [pausing]....but you know what I mean, tipping off Mr. Connelly could have been a very big mistake. When you get to the U.S tomorrow, you can straighten things out. Now let's go over the time line of Connelly's dealing in stolen art work once more, he replied.

Specialist Boudreau indicates that the first rumors of stolen artwork surfaced in three cities Berlin, Paris, and Prague late last year. Using the wall charts he explains that the identified stolen art works had been considered lost for the last 60 years and found them listed in their missing art files.

"Our assumption is that the works were the cream of Hitler's confiscated booty from the War. And more important, we believe Connelly has more pieces than the three that surfaced," he stated.

Inspector Bitterman listened intently as Boudreau continued his overview.

"We know from Hitler's' special catalogues which artworks were his favorites. What we don't know is how Rankin Connelly came to find them." He then added.

"We also don't know how he got them out of Europe...." Alderman interjected.

Bitterman noted that in checking the records of U.S. customs there was no record of any shipments by Connelly from Europe to the U.S.

What this tells us is that Connelly has kept the stolen art work somewhere here in Europe." Bitterman surmised.

"You're right Inspector, but looking at the time line [pointing at the schematic on the wall] it appears that if Connelly is the center of this case.....he could have kept the works anywhere in Europe and avoided the attention of U.S. Customs," Alderman noted.

"Exactly my point Alderman......and that's your assignment with Mr. Connelly. Find out the how and the why, and if necessary get him back here for interrogation." Inspector Bitterman responds.

He adds, "Now get your files together and let me know as soon as you find out what's going on in Savannah, Florida."

"Perhaps you mean Georgia" Alderman suggests.

"Right, right......Georgia.....like the song!" Bitterman retorts.

Chapter Seven

The Discovery Story

In preparation for the meeting with Interpol and the Metropolitan Police, Connelly continued his briefing of Weinstein early the next morning.

Over breakfast, he recapped the session the night before and then told Ms. Weinstein of what happened after hiring Ms. Marshall. They both thought there could be a possible breakthrough in understanding the map and documents left by his father.

Connelly said that sometime after dissevering the map and documents, Ms. Marshall, suggested hiring one of her former associates, an attorney in Germany. It was agreed that she would only give him the possible location of the property noted on the map but not any other information.

After a few months, the attorney contacted Ms. Marshall and said he had found a place, which might well match the description given him.

He described the property as abandoned and was a run down farm on a small number of hectares. No one had lived in it as long as anyone could remember. Also, and most important, the local village government was happy to have someone interested in it.

Rankin told Weinstein that at the time he thought if the property turned out to be the mysterious place noted on the map, he would jump at the chance to buy it.

Marshall interjected that she had heard of the nearby village called Mitterwald from her parents as a child. She noted that it was on the same train line, which was used during the War by the Nazis to send people to the concentration camp at Ebersee, Austria.

She said she thought it could be a match for the description of the map's location...on a train line...an abandoned farm...with buildings right near the train tracks.

Rankin continued by saying that it all seemed to be coming together at that point. So shortly after getting confirmation from Ms. Marshall's German Attorney about the property, they set off for Germany and Austria.

He then provided a quick overview of the search to Ms. Weinstein. He told about the incident with the late night shoot out of the car's tires and finding the threatening note.

Weinstein was most interested in this part of the story as she tried to connect the dots between that incident and Interpol's interest in Connelly and stolen artwork.

Connelly told Weinstein the details about the search for and the discovery of the artwork in the bunker. He noted that finding the bunker was almost not to be, until their luck turned for the better. The creaking floor and the trap door revealed the treasures buried more than sixty years ago near the end of the war.

Weinstein then inquired what they did with the artwork found in the bunker and if they took any of it with them, when they left.

Rankin said they hadn't taken any works, but they did uncrate all the art found in the bunker, and took digital photographs of each piece of art.

He also noted that he knew of an art reproduction center in China, which he considered using to make copies of the originals from the digital photos.

She inquired about that as well, and Rankin said that if anything happened to the artwork, he at least would have a record of its existence.

He said that before their departure from the bunker property they closed up the place. They made sure to leave the barn as they found it, in case others might try and figure out what they were up to during their short stay outside of Mitterwald.

Following the discovery, he asked Riva to contact the attorney and purchase the property as originally planned. Rankin indicated the purchase was completed within a month of their arrival back in the U.S.

He continued to give Weinstein an overview of the next few months of his schedule and travels in and out of New York. She was especially interested in the Chinese connection, thinking that it might provide more insight to the Interpol inquiry.

He told her that the tire shooting incident at the farmhouse the first night they were in Austria, made him concerned about vandals or worse, burglars coming onto the property.

The more he thought about the possibility of others finding the artwork in the bunker he decided it would be in his best interest to have copies made of the original and priceless treasures they discovered only months earlier. Since he already had digital images of each work of art taken during the discovery, he sought out an organization, which specialized in reproductions. This led them to the China connection.

Chapter Eight

The China Connection

Rankin told Weinstein that because of his concern regarding the safety of the treasures, he began doing research as to how best to protect the artwork.

He asked a few of his close art dealer contacts about their experience with digital reproductions. They indicated that digitizing original artwork was easy, but the copies might not look exactly like the originals…losing texture, full color, and depth.

One lead however, sounded most intriguing having to do with actual reproduction on treated canvas by Chinese artisans. The process was somewhat of a mystery, but his contact said that the result was most impressive.

"No one can tell the difference between the original and copy," he was told.

Continuing the briefing of Weinstein before the arrival of the Interpol agents, Rankin gave her an overview of their China travels.

"We didn't have time to have the artwork we discovered in the bunker moved, so our best alternative was to make exact copies of it, which led us to China," he began. He then told the following story.

Not wanting to get lost in a busy city like Shanghai, we had ordered a car and driver to take us to the location. It was located in the industrial part of the city in a non-descript looking building.

With some trepidation, we walked through the buildings entrance to meet the reproductive art center's director Mr. Chuang Lee, a very polite Chinese man in his forties wearing casual clothes.

The room was filled with people scurrying around, some very busy painting at a host of easels with others on computers, images on large screens with classical music playing in the background.

Mr. Lee welcomed us and said he was most pleased to have received interest in the work of his company "Original Reproductions LTD."

I noted how impressive the place looked and especially the group of artisans he had working there. One was working on a Monet, and was an exact reproduction….the color, the lighting, and the brush strokes down to the exact detail of the original. It was most impressive.

Mr. Lee said they worked very hard to please their customers, and believed he could be of service to the Foundation.

I then explained what I wanted by presenting the digital photographs contained in the CD's I had made specifically for this project. I said the Foundation had a number of rare paintings, which because of their value, our insurance company wanted reproductions made.

I gave him a written agreement that the transaction was to be a complete secret, and that I would be paying in cash. I also said that it was of utmost importance that no one ever learned of the reproductions being requested by the Foundation.

At first Mr. Lee seemed puzzled by my request as he said everything produced for clients in his organization was always held in complete confidence and never shared with any authorities.

He added that the disk would be returned with the artwork. Of course, I made sure the encrypted disk could not be copied.

Mr. Lee assured us of the results we could expect and said even the original artists would have a most difficult time seeing any difference between their masterpiece and the reproductions.

In ending his story about the reproductions Rankin mentioned to Weinstein that right after that trip he met again with her boss Robert Vestry III in his New York City law offices.

During the discussion with Vestry, Rankin mentioned having copies of the originals made in China. Vestry asked if he brought them with him to the U.S. Rankin said that hadn't, because it was easier to have them shipped to a location in Europe, where he would have easier access to them.

"After Vestry expressed interest in the copying process, I told him that even the frames were exactly the same on the original works," Rankin said.

"I told him that even if Vermeer were alive he couldn't tell the difference." he continued.

Chapter Nine

The Testimony

After taking a short break, the conversation between Connelly, his attorney Azure Weinstein, and Riva Marshall continued.

Weinstein wondered if Interpol knew about the reproductions and Connelly said no...only four people knew; himself, Marshall, Vestry and of course Mr. Lee.

At that point, Weinstein said they needed a specific game plan to make sure Interpol doesn't pursue charges for possession of stolen artwork. She noted that the Interpol agents would be very determined to find something that will justify their investigation and their travels to Savannah.

Rankin responded when he appeared before the Senate Committee on Insurance and Banking a month or so ago, he laid out a good argument against Interpol's recent interest in his activities, never thinking it could be a defense against charges of theft.

"Why did you work one into your testimony?" Weinstein asked. "I thought the Committee was only interested in the how the insurance industry was handling claims from heirs to Holocaust victims?"

"That was just part of their investigation," Connelly responded. "They also wanted to know about the existence of stolen art in most of our leading museums...here and in other countries. So I took advantage of the moment to inform the Committee members of the 'Lost Goods Statutes'."

"As you know," Rankin said, "The committee chairman, our great Senator from New York, Charles Goldenson invited me to appear. I understand your firm also has represented him on various legal matters. So, I figured his committee hearing might be a good forum to set the stage for the hidden treasures saga."

Rankin then pulled out of his briefcase a copy of the transcript of the Committee hearing and handed it to Weinstein. It read as follows:

THE CONGRESSIONAL COMMITTEE HEARING ON ART MUSEUMS AND ARTS FOUNDATIONS

The eight members of the committee met to discuss possession of art works with questionable provenance. Invited to sit at the witness table were six representatives of leading U.S. Museums and Art Foundations.

SENATOR GOLDENSON

Good morning ladies and gentlemen, on behalf of the members we thank you for agreeing to appear before the Committee on Insurance and Banking.

As you are aware when we invited you to participate in our investigation, our main purpose was to determine if all avenues have been exhausted in determining the provenance of the artwork collected by your museums and foundations.

Basically we want to know if the art work stolen during World War II by the Nazis has found its way into your collections and what you have done to find the rightful owners.

Secondly, many insurance claims have been filed and ignored by leading insurance companies by heirs of Holocaust victims.

The companies have hidden behind a clause in the small print of the insurance they sold requiring death certificates or written records to prove the deaths of their family members.

In addition they have denied claims of lost property that was taken from their relatives who were then sent to concentration camps.

SENATOR PUG JENKINS

Mr. Chairman, point of order. A very important vote on an important piece of legislation is to take place this morning, and many members of this committee may take leave of the hearing, once the call is made.

SENATOR GOLDENSON

Yes, my esteemed colleague from Georgia, the chair will certainly understand if members are required to leave. We will then take a short adjournment at that point.

Now if our witnesses would introduce themselves I would then ask that the representative of Art Foundations begin the testimony.

Each of the six representatives then introduces themselves and their affiliation. Included are John Desire' of the New York Museum of Contemporary Art; Antoine Regions of the Los Angeles Art

Museum; Thomas Strube of the Association of Museum Curators; Nigel Whitehead of the Boston Modern Museum of Art; Sayer Weissell of the Jewish Center For War Restitution; and Rankin Connelly, of the Connelly Arts Foundation.

SENATOR GOLDENSON

Our first witness is Rankin Connelly, President of the Connelly Art Foundation, from New York City.

Welcome Mr. Connelly.

Good morning Mr. Chairman and members of the Insurance and Banking Committee. My participation in your inquiry is not as a spokesperson on behalf of Arts Foundations as a group. However since I am president of one of the top five private funders of the arts in the country, I will speak from that position.

SENATOR GOLDENSON

Understood Mr. Connelly, now will you give the committee some insight as to your research of artwork ownership, which may have been collected by our leading museums since World War II.

CONNELLY

Our Foundation is helping to fund the newly established "Arts For the Rightful Heirs" project. Our mission is to list all known works of art which may have been stolen or purchased at a below market value by Nazi leadership during the War.

SENATOR GOLDENSON

And how do you disseminate the information about the project and have you had any success with it?

CONNELLY

We established a website BunkerTreasures.com which lists all known stolen works and in whose possession they were kept. It has been a tremendous undertaking, but to date we've returned more than a hundred works to the rightful heirs. Our Foundation is also cooperating with the "International Foundation for Art Search" and its theft services.

SENATOR GOLDENSON

That is quite impressive Mr. Connelly even in light of the fact that thousands of pieces of art were stolen during the war.

CONNELLY

Much of the list comes from various governments' archives, which grew out of the "Washington Conference on Holocaust-Era Assets." There is also a stolen arts registry called "Trace" which in the late 1990's estimated that there are at least 100,000 works of art missing from countries of Nazi occupation during the war.

SENATOR GOLDENSON

Tell us more about the "Conference on Holocaust-Era Assets," Mr. Connelly.

CONNELLY

This conference took place much before our Foundation was established, but in developing the Rightful Heirs project we did a great deal of research. We found that in 1998 forty-four nations and thirteen nongovernmental organizations met formally to discuss challenges and problems posed by unsettled questions of assets, including art and art objects.

SENATOR GOLDENSON

Besides information for your Rightful Heirs project, what came out of that symposium?

CONNELLY

There was a consensus to use eleven principles with respect to the Nazi confiscated art works. I have provided to the Committee a list of those principals as part of my testimony before you today.

SENATOR GOLDENSON

Thank you Mr. Connelly, yes we do have the eleven principals as part of each Committee members briefing papers.

CONNELLY

In addition, I would like to add a comment for the Committee's consideration, which is not in my prepared remarks.

Recently, I became personally interested in the subject of art theft. Of course the Connelly Arts Foundation has and is continuing to adhere to all the principals of the Rightful Heirs Project.

However there is one, which has been called into question with certain legal authorities. That one is number nine on your listing.

SENATOR GOLDENSON

Yes, I see it. Pertaining to art work that was confiscated by the Nazis but whose rightful owners cannot be identified, is that right?

CONNELLY

Yes, that one in particular is important to all of the Museums and art collectors around the world, because of statutes of limitations. The conferees agreed with the statutes of limitation except that no statutes of limitations should apply to Nazi stolen artwork.

SENATOR GOLDENSON

Are you aware of the U.S. Governments reparations for taking some of the Nazi stolen goods back to the U.S. after the war?

CONNELLY

Yes, I believe you are referring to the property located on the "Gold Train" as it was called...which had property stolen in Hungary and was unloaded in Werfen, Austria after the war. Parke-Bernet Galleries in New York sold much of that artwork in June 1948. Some fifty-seven years later, the U.S. Government reached agreement with the representatives of the Hungarian Jewish community to make restitution.

SENATOR GOLDENSON

So even the U.S. Government decisions after the war were somehow tainted by the Nazi thefts.

CONNELLY

Yes, according to documentation, since then our government has agreed to pay $25.5 million in compensation, with an additional $500,000 for the preservation of documents associated with the "Gold Train", and to declassify any remaining documents related to the "Gold Train".

SENATOR PUG JENKINS

Mr. Chairman an observation and a question for Mr. Connelly.

SENATOR GOLDENSON

Yes, Senator Jenkins please proceed.

SENATOR PUG JENKINS

That is all well and most interesting, but I was personally wondering if would comment on any of your own involvement in stolen artwork. I have heard from a few of my constituents in the Chatham County Police Department that you might have information on that subject.

CONNELLY

Senator, I am not sure what your sources have told you, but you can be assured that the Foundation and me personally adhere to all standards of ethics regarding the subject being discussed here today.

At this point there are rumblings in the audience and photographers are beginning to shoot photos.

SENATOR JENKINS

Well, I'm glad to hear about that Mr. Connelly and do appreciate your willingness to appear before the Committee in light of any dark cloud of aspersions which might have been suggested by a few interested parties in the lovely state of Georgia.

CONNELLY

I am not aware of any dark clouds in the sunny State of Georgia, but I do know that the Georgia Institute for Art and Design has been most receptive to grants made by the Connelly Arts Foundation, and the leadership of that fine institution is playing an integral part in the Rightful Heirs project.

SENATOR PUG JENKINS

Thank you for that information Mr. Connelly, I stand corrected, as I must have been given misinformation information. [Pause] That is all Mr. Chairman.

SENATOR GOLDENSON

Thank you for the acknowledgment Senator Jenkins, the Committee only wants to deal in facts.

Mr. Connelly I know of you are held in very high regard in the arts world, and on behalf of my constituents and those of my fellow Senators, we appreciate your leadership and integrity in pursing the Rightful Heirs Project.

CONNELLY

Thank you Senator Goldenson.   Before concluding my testimony I would like to add one further point for the Committee's consideration.

SENATOR GOLDENSON

Yes, please proceed.

CONNELLY

There are already Lost Goods Statutes on the books of our various levels of government.

If the Committee in its deliberations believes new laws are needed, I call your attention to existing statutes, which provide the following protections.

Generally title to the found property is vested after a certain period of time; the statutes encourage honesty in finders by providing penalties for not complying with the statutes; they also provide protection to the finder; and provide a reasonable method of uniting goods with their true owners.

At this point a bell rings calling most of the Committee members to a vote in an adjacent chamber.

SENATOR GOLDENSON

Thank you Mr. Connelly for the additional information. You are also now excused from further testimony and with that we will adjourn until this afternoon.

After reading the testimony before the Senate Committee, Weinstein then told Rankin that it was a stroke of genius to bring up before the committee and a national audience about the Statutes of Limitations.

"This will certainly go a long way to convince the local police and Interpol that even if you did possess stolen art work, it would be very difficult to connect the dots between what you have and any that might now be circulating around the art world," she said.

At that point the phone rings and before Connelly can answer it, Weinstein quickly gets up and takes the phone from its side table position.

She raises her hand toward Connelly in a "stop" motion thinking it could be from Police Headquarters, as she answers the phone.

"Hello, Ms. Weinstein speaking........ah yes, he is here but not available at the moment. May I tell him whose calling? Oh I see Inspector, [pause] yes, we can be there at 10 a.m. tomorrow.....Ok see you then....and by the way Inspector unless you or Interpol are prepared to make charges against Mr. Connelly, we are leaving Savannah tomorrow evening," Weinstein warns.

Chapter Ten

Interpol Inquiry

The next morning, Connelly, Marshall and Weinstein are picked up at the hotel in a limo, which had been arranged by Weinstein to transport the trio to Police Headquarters.

After they arrive at the Metropolitan Police office of Inspector Forsythe, he escorts them into an adjacent conference room. Already seated at the large conference table are Interpol agents Alderman and Boudreau, who rise as the others enter the room.

Inspector Forsythe then introduces the individuals and notes that the Interpol agents have just arrived that morning from their flight from France.

He also said this was just an exploratory meeting and not an interrogation, pointing out that Ms. Marshall was welcome to stay as an observer and if she wanted to add any direct information it would be welcomed.

After the exchange of pleasantries the questioning begins with Alderman saying their interest centers upon stolen artwork from World War II, which they understand, could be in Connelly's possession

Weinstein interjects that they seem to be getting way ahead of themselves since there is no evidence of any connection between her client Mr. Connelly and stolen art work.

Alderman responds by saying that Interpol believes Mr. Connelly has either found or purchased art work that was stolen by the Nazis during the War.....and that they are in Savannah to learn how he came to have it and where it is now located.

Connelly then interrupts and offers to give some background to the two Interpol agents and Inspector Forsythe. He notes that it might clear up a number of their questions and assumptions.

Agent Boudreau then tells Connelly that they didn't travel all night to listen to his stories...but they are only interested in facts and the whereabouts of the artwork.

"Well Mr. Boudreau and Mr. Alderman...and you too Mr. Forsythe, I want each of you to understand that I am here only because I want this matter cleared up and cleared up now. Do you get my drift?" he retorts angrily.

Connelly leans forward toward both of the Interpol agents and addresses them directly.

"So let's get down to just facts and I think you will be able to fill in that pad of yours with quite a bit of information if you pay attention to what I have to say...with no interruptions and no questions until I am finished. Understand?" he says.

Agents Alderman and Boudreau are taken aback by his forceful tone, but nod in agreement.

Connelly then relates to the Interpol Agents and Inspector Forsythe the following story.

Near the end of World War II, my father had been on active duty when the allies moved through France and on into Germany and Austria. He was a platoon leader on the front lines with the 103rd Infantry.

During a skirmish in late March, 1945 he came upon a Nazi train which had been carrying a mysterious cargo.

I found out recently the Nazi train had been unloaded of art treasures just before my father's platoon attacked it and taking out those on board.

After the train had been hit by mortar shells and blown up, my father was one of the first soldiers on the scene.

From the notes written in his diary, I learned that when he surveyed the destruction of the blown up and still smoldering train cars he turned as he hears one of his soldiers yelling to him. He's called over to the area where the soldier finds an open pouch with documents falling out of it.

He picks up the documents and then he begins to stuff some of the documents in his jacket but stops and unfolds one of them noticing that it is a map.

His diary then noted that he wanted to get it to his 103rd Infantry Headquarters, thinking that they would definitely be interested in reading the documents and in especially checking out the map.

As he began to walk away from the fallen Nazi officer from whom Connelly took the documents, the Nazi suddenly pulls out his pistol and shoots my father in the back. Although wounded, my father turned around and shot the Nazi.

At that point Rankin stopped and looked around the room and said, "My father must have then fallen unconscious to the ground, because that is all that was written about that episode in his diary."

He then continued to tell the Interpol agents and Inspector Forsythe the rest of the story about what happened to his father.

The documents never made it back to headquarters as his father had planned. The reason being that shortly after this incident he was shipped directly back to the States along with all of his personal belongings. Fortunately he made a recovery shortly after we had declared victory over the Nazis.

With the war ended, he must have seen no point in doing anything with the map and documents which were mixed in with his personal belongings. They were put away until his death more than a year ago.

When Connelly finished, Alderman remarked that he told a most interesting story and it might even make a good movie, but it doesn't tell them anything about his involvement in dealing with stolen artwork.

Now very upset with the lack of understanding by the Interpol agent, Connelly remarked that the story of his father and the German documents is exactly why he volunteered to stay in Savannah and meet with them.

"The map in question led me to a bunker specifically authorized by Hitler to store the cream of his art collection. As far as I have been able to ascertain, the works were probably stolen during the War from unwitting individuals and art dealers." Connelly said.

Now quite surprised by Connelly's admission of his finding these buried treasures, Boudreau asked how

Connelly could have uncovered artwork buried since 1945.

He repeated again that his father knew the war had ended and having recovered from his wounds....he put the Nazi documents away not realizing what information they contained. He added a few pages from his diary, which described what happened that day in 1945.

"As far as I can ascertain, he put them in a safe deposit box and never looked at them again. They sat there until his death in early 2009." Rankin added.

At this point Forsythe, who had been quiet during the entire morning, chimed in the questioning. He said that it was hard for him to believe that his father would never had interest in learning where the map might lead.

"You didn't know my father," Rankin responded. "He was a strong willed man, someone who never looked back. Both the war and incident at the Nazi train had a major effect on him.

Alderman wanting to pursue the discovery of the bunker asked Connelly whether it was at this point that he began to search for what lay behind the mysterious Nazi documents.

Rankin told him no, that it was much later that he started to unravel the mystery of the map. His first priority was getting the Connelly Arts Foundation organized. This was the final wish of his father.

It was after this initial start up that he began in earnest to do research behind the documents and map, which he had hoped would then led to uncovering the Nazi and specifically Hitler's hidden art collection.

Boudreau asked about when he actually found the bunker and thus the stolen artwork.

Recounting the time period, Connelly said it took a while before he embarked on unraveling the mysterious map. He noted that during the start up phase of the foundation he was fortunate to hire someone with knowledge of the area where his father found the map.

"In addition to my understanding of the language, she could also speak German," Rankin added as he turned toward Ms. Marshall and nodded.

"Together Ms. Marshall and I began the search and were successful in discovering what the map had kept hidden for more than 60 years," he added.

"Mr. Connelly did you discover any other contraband such as jewels, gold, or currency during your search?" Alderman asked.

"Not necessarily contraband, but when we discovered the art work, we did find something else that may turn out to be of historic importance to the Russian Government," Connelly responded.

He then continued by saying that in the research they conducted about that era, they found that the German Army at the specific order of Hitler took The Amber Room from the Russian Imperial Palace during the occupation of Russia in 1941.

The Germans then put The Amber Room back together piece by piece and put it on display at a castle in Konigsberg.

Forsythe interjected "I thought the Germans hid The Amber Room after it was dismantled in Russia."

Rankin responded by saying when they first took it from the Russians they moved it to Konigsberg and later the Nazis again dismantled it and packed all the amber panels in crates during January 1945. "They then moved it and it has never been found since that time", he added.

"How is this connected to the bunker?" Forsythe asked, now very interested in where all this was leading.

"Once we opened the bunker we found some other documents which might shed light on the mystery of The Amber Room's disappearance," Connelly responded.

Boudreau then told Connelly that the bunker story might be plausible, but Interpol's interest at this point was in the stolen artwork, not the whereabouts of The Amber Room.

"There have been so many discoveries of its location that it has taken on a mysterious life of its own. You are now "marcher sur la glace mince" as they say in France." Boudreau said.

"Come again Agent Boudreau, in English!" Forsythe asked.

"As we say in France, Mr. Connelly is now 'treading on thin ice' Inspector.'" Boudreau responded.

During the questioning, Weinstein observed the volleying back and forth, but after a few more questions she raised her voice and said. "Listen up," as she turned toward the two Interpol agents

Alderman and Boudreau, "we have had enough of this for the time being, and unless you are prepared to file charges and go through the extradition process, this get together has just ended."

Now looking directly at Inspector Forsythe she added, "you know Mr. Connelly has not dealt in stolen artwork either from the war or anytime after that. So we are out of here now," she exclaimed.

Then both Forsythe and Alderman begin speaking at the same time

"No, you just wait a minute, Ms. Weinstein, Chatham County may file charges as soon as........."

Alderman cutting off Inspector Forsythe in mid sentence, Alderman then interjected, "Excuse me Inspector, but let me set the record straight for Ms. Weinstein. We understand German authorities are at this point most interested in securing an indictment against Mr. Connelly for possession of stolen artwork."

Weinstein then retorts, "Well while you are arguing about jurisdiction, we will adjourn to our hotel, and prepare to leave for New York."

As Connelly, Marshall, and Weinstein stand up and begin walking toward the door, Forsythe makes an offer to let them leave under one condition.

"Just a moment.....we agree to let you leave on the condition you stay in Savannah one more day so this can be sorted out between Interpol, the Germans and ourselves," he indicates.

"We agreed with that request yesterday" Weinstein responds, "and let's face it, you still don't have any grounds for keeping Mr. Connelly here......so we are leaving from the Savannah airport this evening."

The trio then walks out of the conference room, leaving Inspector Forsythe, Agents Alderman and Boudreau fuming.

As they leave the Police Headquarters, Rankin waves to the limo driver who had been standing by awaiting their departure.

Riva then asks Rankin if it would be okay for her to meet them back at the hotel, as she wanted to pick up some personal items before they head back to New York.

"I will meet both of you back at the hotel....promise I won't be gone very long" she mentions as she kisses Rankin on the cheek and waves goodbye and heads towards the downtown shopping area.

As she walks quickly away, Rankin notices an unusual site down the street. It is a Humvee painted in green camouflaged colors, the kind of vehicle used by the U. S. in military operations.

Thinking back to his days as a Special Forces member, he shakes his head and wonders if the government is trying to make up the deficit by selling used military vehicles.

He and Weinstein then get in the limo and it leaves the Police Headquarters and speeds away.

Just as quickly, the camouflaged Humvee also pulls away from the curb and follows the limo.

All of a sudden, the Humvee pulls along side of the limo and cuts directly into it, forcing it to swerve.

The limo speeds ahead and again the Humvee gets along side of it and rams it but this time the limo's front wheel catches the curb, spins and then flips over to rest leaning up against an art gallery window.

Chapter Eleven

Hospital Surprise

Both Connelly and Weinstein were rushed to the hospital along with the limo driver shortly after the accident. A number of witnesses came forward when the police arrived on the scene to give statements.

Only a few witnesses however mentioned seeing the Humvee. People scattered when they saw the limo flip over, landing against the lower brick wall, which was the facing of the art gallery. Fortunately no one other than the passengers was hurt.

After arriving at the hospital the trio were given head to toe examinations by the attending doctors. All three were dazed by the limo rolling over and over before landing against the building. By the time they reached the hospital they were groggy but conscious.

Later in the afternoon, after Connelly was put in a private recovery room a female doctor came in, holding x-rays and a chart. Weinstein had already been discharged suffering only slight abrasions on her head. She was seated next to the bed, her head bandaged.

"Well, well Mr. Connelly good news. No broken bones and no life threatening injuries, but you might want to take it easy for a while. I'd say the luck of the Irish was with you this afternoon," the doctor said.

"And Ms. Weinstein, seems as if you survived with only slight abrasions on your forehead. Very fortunate, but please leave the bandage on your head for a few days." she added.

Weinstein said it sounded OK to her and that both of them could count their blessings that no one was killed in the accident.

At that point, Forsythe enters the room just as Weinstein is finishing her sentence about not being killed in the accident.

"That was no accident Ms. Weinstein. You all were the target of foul play by someone who wanted to either kill or send a strong message to you," he stated.

"What do you mean Inspector?

Forsythe introduced himself to the doctor and asked if he could speak to the patients in private, noting it was routine police business.

"Actually I was just finishing up and have to continue my rounds, it has been a busy afternoon already," she said. Then added, "Mr. Connelly, I want you to stay the night, and if there are no complications, you may leave tomorrow morning."

The doctor then leaves the room, taking the x-rays, and signs the clipboard charts hanging at the end of Connelly's bed.

Forsythe then inquired about the condition of Ms. Marshall wondering if she was in the adjacent room.

Connelly replied no, and told Forsythe that she was very lucky that she didn't come with them in the limo, but went to do some personal shopping.

"I spoke with her this afternoon and let her know we were okay, but not to come here in case we were all a target," Connelly added.

He then mentioned to Azure to have Ms. Marshall cancel their flights and rebook them for late morning the next day.

A discussion then ensued about whether this was an accident or a deliberate attempt on their lives.

"It doesn't take a great deal of investigative experience to conclude someone is trying to rub you out," Forsythe said.

"Rub out?' Weinstein asked.

"Well that might not be the politically correct phrase to use, let me just say the driver of the other vehicle was trying to cause significant bodily harm to you," he responded.

Connelly asked if the police had any information on who was driving the other vehicle. Forsythe said that they didn't yet but that vehicle in question was found about ten miles away, parked at the airport.

Connelly said he was impressed that the Chatham Metro Police could work that fast in finding the vehicle.

It was then that Forsythe said that airport security noticed it was not the typical Humvee. It was a specially prepared vehicle that is customized in Chatham County by Backriver Industries for use by the military. It had been reported stolen yesterday from the factory's proving grounds.

Connelly inquired whether the police thought that whomever was behind the attempt had flown out of the airport.

"My gut feeling is that they did not. I think the Humvee was left there to throw us off their trail. We're checking with car rental agencies to see all those who might have rented a car between this morning and afternoon just in case", he responded.

Both Connelly and Weinstein then asked if the police still thought the suspects were still in Savannah.

Forsythe said that it appeared to him that someone just wanted to hurt Connelly and is sending a message, otherwise they could have killed him in a different fashion. He added that just in case, police protection would be provided as long as they stayed in Savannah.

"I do appreciate that gesture Inspector, but we're leaving tomorrow for New York. We are days behind in our other business obligations," Rankin said.

"Listen Mr. Connelly this whole episode is very serious to me and our department. This is especially so, now that we found some papers in the Humvee which mentions something about The Amber Room", Forsythe said.

Connelly in a surprised reaction said "What the hell?"

Forsythe then volunteered the information that in checking the vehicle for fingerprints, one of their investigators found a folder with news stories about the search for the Amber Room...and some other documents in German.

'Oh my God, Rankin, could it be the.." Weinstein blurted out. Connelly interrupted her saying "Hold it Azure….let's discuss this later.

Forsythe's somewhat taken aback by Rankin's statement responds, "What do you mean later. How about the present? If this is connected to our investigation, I want answers and want them now!"

Connelly agrees but only if whatever is said from that point on is off the record.

"No can do." Forsythe responds. "You might not be in New York, but down here we play by the rules. Nothing you say is 'off the record', nothing."

Weinstein then reminds Connelly that he does not have to respond to any of the Inspector's questions.

Forsythe then backs off by saying that his interest is to "just try and find out who and why someone is trying to kill y'all."

Then a discussion ensues between the three of them regarding the documents found in the abandoned Humvee, and if there are any leads on who drove the vehicle at the time of the incident downtown.

Forsythe responds in the negative and says his gut feeling is that the culprits are still in the area. He adds, "They didn't exactly finish what they started out to do!"

He reminds them that they are still in serious danger and does not want them to leave Savannah until the police can get a better handle on the situation.

"I understand your concerns, Connelly interjects, "but we still need to leave and at this point I would feel a lot better in New York than in Savannah...nothing personal of course."

At this point Forsythe knows it's a losing battle to keep Connelly and Weinstein in Savannah. He acknowledges that there is no legal basis for him to hold someone who is only "considered" in possession of stolen artwork.

"Our friends at Interpol on the other hand, are a different story." Forsythe states.

Once more Connelly assures the Inspector that he has never dealt in stolen anything and his sole aim at this point is to get to the bottom of the whole mess.

Chapter Twelve

Austria Revisited

After the Interpol interrogation and attempt on his life, Connelly left Savannah wondering what was going to happen next.

The trip was supposed to be a positive experience in giving the commencement address to the new graduates of the Southern Institute of Art and Design in Savannah. He was very much looking forward to announcing that the Connelly Foundation was going to award a full scholarship annually to the Institute for an aspiring artist.

It never entered his mind that he would be under investigating for dealing in stolen artwork, let alone is the subject of an inquiry by the Stolen Art Work Task Force of Interpol.

The three days spent in Savannah at the request, no the demand of the Chatham County Metropolitan Police put him way behind on his pressing Foundation business schedule.

Connelly was shaken by the attempt on his life. But he was having a most difficult time in trying to connect the dots between that incident and the police finding documents in the stolen Humvee pertaining to The Amber Room.

Someone knew a lot more than he wanted to admit about his discovery a year earlier of the treasures buried more than a half century ago by Hitler's minions. Who could it be he wondered?

He traced his movements from the time he first learned of the mysterious map and the reading the torn pages from his father's wartime diary. He thought it best at this point to revisit the Vestry Law firm in New York to try and sort things out.

After confirming an appointment with Robert Vestry, he pulled together the notes he had made in an effort to fully explore the situation he faced.

After exchanging pleasantries with Vestry, who invited Weinstein to sit in on the meeting he recalled the statement about his father not wanting to have the map lead to an unwanted destiny.

"None of us could have ever imagined that someone driving a Humvee in Savannah would be the culprit that would try to send you to that 'unwanted destiny'," Vestry said.

"Yes, it does sound very strange. A lot has happened in the year you and I sat here going over my father's will, but I could never have imagined what has happened since then," Connelly responded.

The whereabouts of Ms. Marshall was the question on the mind of Azure Weinstein, who hadn't been seen since she left Savannah the week before along with Connelly.

He said that just after they returned to New York from Savannah, she was called back to Germany unexpectedly because of the failing health of her mother. And while she's there, she was to do some more research and meet with the war historian, Klaus Reinhardt in Berlin.

Vestry then told Connelly that Ms. Weinstein had filled him in on his testimony to the to the Senate Banking and Insurance Committee's hearings on art theft and restitution.

"It was good that you contacted Senator Goldenson and volunteered to testify before the committee." he said.

"I will say Rankin, not only would your father have been proud of you for how you handled Senator Jenkins, but that you also worked into your testimony about the unclaimed property statute." he added.

Weinstein commented how impressive his testimony was as she watched the faces of the Senators as he was testifying.

"They had no idea of the scope you and the Foundation were playing in the stolen art work area. You were amazing Rankin," Weinstein said.

Connelly thanked them both for their complements but said the question remained about how Interpol got involved in the inquiry and more importantly who is behind wanting to do him in. "The search for the Amber Room pales in comparison to what I am up against at the moment," he added.

"Pales….good pun, Rankin," Weinstein said.

"From a legal standpoint," Vestry commented, "I don't believe after your testimony about trying to find the rightful owners of the treasures you found in Austria, you have much to worry about. I don't have a clue however about who is trying to send you such a drastic message or make sure you don't proceed," Vestry added.

Connelly replied that he remembers from his days at West Point, to never assume anything and always be ready for the worst case scenario.

"Words to live by Rankin," Vestry commented. "But, what happens next might test that philosophy."

In reviewing his plan to return to Austria with Vestry and Weinstein, Connelly said that he was going to remove the artwork from the bunker. He also said he wanted to meet with Interpol in an attempt to clear up any misunderstanding about the accusation of dealing in stolen artwork.

"Excellent idea Rankin, the sooner you get that Interpol business behind you the better. But one final word of advice, don't reveal to anyone including Interpol, the location of the bunker and its treasure. You must take every precaution not to draw their attention to its location," Vestry cautioned.

Vestry then changed the subject to the threats that have been made in an attempt to help Connelly narrow down the possibilities.

"I know you have made different contacts in Europe," Vestry said. "A number of people know you are looking for the Amber Room, but does anyone stand out in your mind that would want you dead?

Weinstein chimed in that if Connelly reviewed his various European travel experiences with them perhaps it might prompt an answer to Vestry's question.

He noted that in his travels with Ms. Marshall, they did meet up with some interesting and perhaps unsavory characters. Reviewing the people they met with he mentioned Justov in Russia, Steinbacker in Vienna, Barlinger in Linz, and D'Alivia in Salzburg.

"You two certainly got around," Weinstein noted, "but you didn't mention the men outside Mitterwald near where you found the bunker."

Unaware what happened at the Austrian farmhouse, Vestry inquired about it.

Connelly responded by saying that the two incidents might be connected, but no one knew they were going to the village other than the attorney Marshall had contacted.

"The first evening after we arrived at the property", Connelly said, "someone shot out the tires of our rental car...which we had to have replaced the next day."

He added, "The situation with the tires might have just been a bad joke to scare the two of us away from the farm," Connelly said. "Earlier in the day men in the village whom we asked about the location of the property, laughed about the place being filled with ghosts," he added.

"But Rankin, you didn't mention anything about the written threats left in German," Weinstein said.

"Threats?" Vestry exclaimed.

Connelly then filled Vestry in on the whole episode, leaving out the part of his romantic interlude with Marshall. He told him that there were newspaper clippings with pasted word cutouts saying in effect "you are not wanted here".

Vestry inquired if he then contacted the authorities, and Connelly said they decided not to, so as to avoid calling attention to why they were there and thinking it might have just been a prank by locals.

Vestry said he thought that was the right decision and then asked about the European contacts he made during the travels with Marshall.

In his effort to give Vestry more background information, he highlighted the travels with Marshall some months after the discovery of the hidden bunker treasures.

We first went to Vienna, because we, I mean Ms. Marshall learned that in their National Culture Archives, they had documents pertaining to train movements in Austria by the Germans during the war.

One of the major finds by the Americans were the treasures found in salt mines at Alt Aussee. So we decided to begin our research in Austria.

We drove to Vienna to meet with the minister of the Austrian Cultural Center, Horst Steinbacker.

After our arrival, Mr. Steinbacker greeted us, and we expressed our appreciation for his willingness to help with our research project into World War II documents.

Steinbacker said it was his distinct pleasure to offer his services to the Connelly Art Foundation in this matter. He noted that Austria has an interest in resolving certain left over matters from the war.....after all the Führer, Adolf Hitler, left a black mark on their history.

We said our only interest at the moment was taking a look at their archives as they related to movement of trains near the end of the War.

We then were escorted to a private conference room where Steinbacker had placed a great deal of material on the large table. We then proceeded to comb through an extraordinary number of documents and maps. Whenever we found something useful, we took digital photographs of the relevant material.

We found this trove of Nazi communications and maps incredible, so many documents pointing out not only where the Nazi trains were headed, but troop movements and plans for Germany's Fourth Reich if the Allies failed in their mission against the Nazis.

Marshall found documents pertaining to the disposition of the counterfeiting operation where the Nazis were printing English pound sterling notes. The lake in which the equipment was found...Lake Toplitz wasn't very far from there...only a few hours.

I had learned that the Museum connected to the Austrian Culture Center in Vienna had received 300 pieces of artwork and documents in the past few years. These were donated by the wealthy Barlinger family and had been collected by the family since World War II. I had heard the eldest son of the parents had an obsession with Nazi documents.

It was in these documents that we discovered a reference to the Amber Room in a note signed by Hitler sent to Eigher, one of his closest art collectors.

Marshall got excited then and exclaimed "You're right.....oh my God, Rankin.....look at this...a reference to the Amber Room, and it is signed by Hitler. It's a note to Eigher...one of his art collectors."

Although worn somewhat with age, we were able to determine that it was an order from Hitler in 1945 to move the Amber Room from the Konigsberg Castle, to somewhere toward the Austrian border...and to do it in the strictest confidence and as soon as possible.

We took a number of digital photos of this and accompanying documents; ones which were never uncovered by the Allies or the Russians.

Shortly after this, Steinbacker returned and indicated the Center was closing and insisted we leave as soon as we could gather our belongings.

I asked about the document signed by Hitler, and that is when Steinbacker began to become very defensive. He said he had no knowledge of that particular document being in the collection, and would see to it that it was sent to the authorities in Berlin.

There a repository exists for researchers to comb over Nazi documents in the hope of understanding what happened to the German people before and during the National Socialist Party ruled by Hitler took over control of all phases of German life.

Before leaving, we asked Steinbacker for one last favor, an introduction to the remaining heir to the Ballenger family fortune, Hans Barlinger. He agreed.

After departing Vienna and the Austrian Cultural Center with our interest peaked, we headed toward Linz, which was only a few hours away by car.

The Barlinger Corporation did very well following the war. It received many of the contracts for the reconstruction of German cities infrastructure. The Barlinger Group built most of the sewer lines, water lines, electrical systems, and water purification plants.

Thus the family fortune grew over the decades after the war and all of that was left to their two sons Hans and Rudy.

We arrived at the Barlinger estate early afternoon. The entrance was gated and we had to be let in by the security guard. I have seen opulence before but this property would be near the top of the list of extravagant estates. It reminded me of the properties built for the Rockefellers in upstate New York.

During the drive to Linz we wondered if this was a good idea, considering the hesitancy of Steinbacker to provide the introduction, but we wanted to get a better understanding of what we uncovered at the Austrian Cultural Mission. We were soon to find out.

After being escorted into a museum quality sitting room we were introduced to Hans Barlinger by his social secretary.

He turned out to be a most debonair man in his late forties who spoke with a distinctly British accent. He got right to the point. No pleasantries.

"So Mr. Connelly, Director Steinbacker said you think my deceased brother Rudy had information about the Amber Room...because you found one of Hitler's documents in the Culture Organization's archives?" Barlinger asked, after we were seated in the plush sitting room where he was waiting.

I explained that yes we were interested in the Amber Room information, but more how his brother had come to possess the documents.

"My brother lived and died mysteriously Mr. Connelly," Barlinger replied. "He had a scavenger's mentality about finding what others couldn't and reveling in his success. He was the one who funded the expedition to uncover the counterfeiting paraphernalia which was discovered a few years ago in Lake Toplitz," he added.

Marshall was most interested in Barlinger's British accent since he was Austrian by birth.

Barlinger explained that his parents thought a proper education would be one in Great Britain, so he was sent to a boarding school in the mid sixties, as a child and then matriculated at Oxford.

He said his roots are Austrian but his accent is quite British. He added that his brother Rudy was much older and received his education in Germany. He explained that this accounted for his brother's deep interest in most things German especially the Nazi participation in World War II.

Connelly said that they understood a great deal of the family's artwork collection was donated to the Vienna Museum of Art following his brother's death."

"Quite right Mr. Connelly, when my parents died we shared equally in their estate. Rudy and I split the investments, but he received the artwork and I received the properties," Barlinger chuckled. "And of course after Rudy was killed, his will directed his assets be given to the Vienna Art Museum and the Cultural Organization."

Impressed by the donated collection of the Barlinger family, Connelly said that they had seen some of the collection through the courtesy of Director Steinbacker. "It is a most important group of 17th and 18th Century art," Connelly noted.

Marshall was a bit more to the point when she asked directly about the source of his bother's collection of Nazi documents he secured during his lifetime.

Not missing a beat, Barlinger said his brother's primary contact source was a collector in Berlin....who now lives in Salzburg. His name is Mario D'Alivia.

"An Italian?" Marshall asked.

"Only by ancestry." Barlinger responded, "Actually he is German, born of some questionable heritage. He deals in hard to find documents from the War as well as otherwise confidential materials."

Responding to my request for a contact number or an address for Mr. D'Alivia, Barlinger offered to assist by providing the contact information. He then went to his desk to retrieve it.

"He can be found at this address. Please do not tell him of our meeting....I want nothing to do with him. He is a most unpleasant man...and was a suspect in my brother's death," he said.

After a short while longer, we thanked him for his courtesies and for accepting our request to meet and discuss his brother's collection of Nazi documents.

Following our meeting with Barlinger, we continued on to Salzburg, stopping for dinner along the way. Ms. Marshall also wanted to take a brief walk after all the sitting we did during the day.

We did however want to meet directly with the referral made by Barlinger as soon as possible.

After walking along a very narrow street and following the directions on the notepaper given to us by Barlinger we found the address.

After repeatedly knocking on the nondescript entrance door, we were about to walk away when we heard footsteps behind us. Turning around we saw a small thin man who spoke with a German accent.

I assumed it was D'Alivia, but waited for the man to introduce himself, which he did shortly after opening the entrance door.

He called us by name and I asked how he knew who we were.

D'Alivia responded by saying "sources Mr. Connelly, I deal in sources and in my business it is always best to stay one step ahead to avoid surprises. Come in please."

We followed D'Alivia down a dimly lit hallway to a room, which was lined with volumes of notebooks and three ring binders, but no books. We were motioned to sit at a large conference table with D'Alivia continuing to walk around the room in a nervous pattern.

He asked how he could be of service and we told him we were doing research on what happened to the Amber Room at the end of the war when it was moved from Konigsberg.

D'Alivia then just laughed and said many others had tried over the years to find it including the Russians who want it back.

Marshall volunteered we knew of Hitler's orders to have it removed from Konigsberg and shipped to somewhere in Austria.

D'Alivia said she was partially correct in that it was moved from Konigsberg in February 1945 but its destination remained a mystery. "Of course many theories abound, such as it was hidden in a salt mine, silver mine and possibly in an abandoned railway tunnel." he added.

I told him we knew of those theories, but our interest was specific to the time period from February until Hitler's suicide in April.

He warned us that we were getting in dangerous territory and that there were people who do not want the Amber Room found. "They will do anything to continue the mystery." He said.

I told him that we both understood the danger, but that it was news to us that there were people who did not want the Amber Room found by anyone other than themselves.

At this point D'Alivia stopped pacing around the room and went to one of the lower shelves in the bookcase and pulls out a scrapbook of newspaper clippings and lays it on the table in front of Connelly and Marshall.

He commented about how many newspaper articles have been written about the search for the Amber panels and called our attention to one article in particular. It was a clipping from the New York Times written as recently as this year.

The Times article was about a serious and expensive undertaking by a Argentinean mine owner, who supposedly had firsthand information given to him by one of the many Nazi SS officers who found his way to South America after the war.

D'Alivia said that these treasure hunters did not find it either, nor would they be happy knowing we have joined the search.

He added that it wasn't the well-funded scavengers who we should be concerned with, but the Russian Government has a strong nationalistic interest in finding the Amber Room.

Marshall told D'Alivia that the Connelly Arts Foundation would be happy to provide the Russians with any information they could obtain about the Amber Room whereabouts.

D'Alivia scoffed at this and asked what in return would the Foundation want from the Russians?

I told him that it was no secret that after the war, the Russians took from Germany thousands of art works and antiquities, which did not belong to the Russians. They called it restitution for the misery and damages caused to their country by the Nazis. Now most of that artwork is in storage in St. Petersburg and Moscow, and it hasn't seen the light of day since the war.

As Connelly finished his review of their Austrian travels he said, "so that in a nutshell was our brief research tour after finding the bunker, except that our last lead...a Professor Reinhardt wasn't available."

Vestry said that he was curious about how D'Alivia knew their names, when only Barlinger knew about their intended visit.

"Very good question," Connelly responded. "Frankly, I was taken by surprise at that, but then again in D'Alivia's circle it is a very close community. But now that you brought it up, you are right, only Barlinger knew where we were headed after our visit."

Weinstein inquired of Connelly his mentioning a Professor Otto Reinhardt as someone he and Riva were supposed to meet while in Germany. She wanted to know how Reinhardt fit into the puzzle?

Vestry then interjected "Oh Ms. Weinstein I don't believe that has any relevance."

Connelly responded that perhaps it does because he was someone that D'Alivia mentioned who also dealt in hard to find Nazi era documents.

"Riva said that he is a professor of history and has written extensively on the art collections of Hitler, Bormann and Herman Goering. I tried to make phone contact but we couldn't locate him." Connelly said.

Weinstein found Connelly's comment interesting and told him so. "So you didn't contact him, but Riva is going to on your behalf?" she asked.

He said yes and that Riva had family business to attend to in Germany, but while there she would continue to try and find Reinhardt and if successful was to meet with him.

"Rankin of more interest to me at this point, is trying to help you through this Interpol inquiry. Let's discuss what they know and how they found out about the treasure trove you found in Austria," Vestry interjected.

He then added, "Does Interpol know where the bunker is located?"

Connelly responded in the negative saying that during the visit to the property they were careful not to call attention to anything pertaining to the bunker. He added that this was the main reason they didn't contact the local authorities when intruders shot out the rental car tires.

"At this point the only people who know the location are you and Azure in addition to Riva and myself," Connelly stated.

"What about the German attorney, you know the one that Riva asked to check out the property?" Weinstein then asked.

Connelly explained that even though the attorney obviously was aware of the location of the property, that he had no knowledge of why they wanted it nor that they found anything of value there.

"Riva and I agreed that we would keep the discovery in complete confidence until I had a chance to check out the statutes of limitations on artwork stolen during the war," Connelly replied.

He then went on to explain how he secured information that he used in his testimony before the Senate Banking and Insurance Committee hearings.

It was during his research of the subject that he learned of the efforts of the various Jewish organizations to locate and return works of art to the heirs of those it was taken from by the Nazis.

He also decided at that point to have the Connelly Arts Foundation take the lead and start the project, "Arts For The Rightful Owners." It said it was from this interest that a website was created to further the projects reach around the world.

"My plan now is to return to Austria while I am in Europe go to Lyon, France and meet with Interpol to clear up the misunderstanding about dealing in stolen art work," Connelly said.

'Excellent idea Rankin," Vestry said. "The sooner you get that Interpol business behind you the better. But again a word of caution, don't reveal to anyone including Interpol, the location of the bunker and its treasure, you must be very cautious."

Then Weinstein added, "Please be very careful Rankin."

Chapter Thirteen

The Interpol Meeting

Within a few days after meeting with Vestry and Weinstein, Connelly heard from Marshall that she was okay, but so far was unable to contact Professor Reinhardt. She did say that her mother was much better, and so happy that she was able to visit her.

Connelly told her that he was traveling to Austria and hoped that they could meet there to discuss Foundation business as well as renew their now long interrupted personal relationship. He told Riva that he missed her very much and that she had given him another reason to feel so lucky, in spite of the recent troubles in Savannah.

He failed to mention his wanting to meet again with Interpol, thinking Riva would get worried about them detaining or worse, arresting him on their home turf in France.

He felt that although he resisted it at first, that his feelings for Riva were growing deeper. A love that he didn't know he could embrace again in his life. His heart wanted to protect Riva from any thoughts of his being the target of someone or some group's ill intentions.

His flight from Liberty International Airport in Newark to the Lyon Airport was most comfortable and smooth. The long flight during the night gave him the chance to catch up on some sleep before his morning meeting at Interpol's offices in Lyon.

After landing, he caught a Taxi and went directly to his hotel in the center part of the historic Lyon to freshen up. He also wanted to gather his thoughts as how best to handle the meeting with Inspector Bitterman, the head of Interpol's Stolen Art Work Task Force. Rankin had heard that he was not an easy man to deal with and had a one-track mind.

Following the meeting in Savannah, agents Boudreau and Alderman were anxiously awaiting the opportunity to question Connelly on their own turf. They knew Connelly had a lot more information than he had shared with them in their Chatham County Metropolitan Police Department Conference Room a few months previously.

Their briefing of Inspector Bitterman on the outcome of that meeting was less than either of them had hoped. To put it bluntly, Inspector Bitterman was pissed and beside himself after they told him of the fiasco in Savannah.

This then would be their opportunity to clear the air with their boss and have Connelly in a position that he wouldn't have his New York attorney advising not to answer their questions.

They believed Connelly was not telling the full story and they wanted to take the opportunity to press him into admitting it.

When Connelly arrived at Interpol's imposing headquarters, he was escorted through the metal detectors, which had become standard equipment in all public safety offices since 9-11. After checking his briefcase as well as patting him down, the on duty security guard escorted him to Inspector Bitterman's office on the third floor of the building.

Surprisingly, he was graciously welcomed by Bitterman who said, "We appreciate you voluntarily coming to see us Mr. Connelly. My associates Specialist Alderman and Boudreau were impressed with your directness in the Savannah interviews and described you as someone who shoots straight."

Alderman said, "perhaps what Inspector Bitterman means is that you are a straight shooter."

"Right, right, sometimes my American slang doesn't translate too well," Bitterman muttered in his German accent.

Nodding his head in agreement, Rankin then said his purpose in Savannah as well as now in their offices is to clear up the misunderstanding about the artwork he found near the Austrian border a year earlier.

Agent Boudreau agreed that would be a good place to begin.

'You have already heard the whole background of how I came into its possession, and my objective is to find the heirs of its rightful owners," Connelly responded.

Alderman then caught Connelly off guard by saying how interesting Connelly's stated objective is to return the stolen art work to its rightful owners, when some of the art has already made its appearance in various cities in Europe.

"Come again?" Connelly said.

"You heard me, we believe the works which you say you have in Austria are now surfacing in various cities in Europe," Alderman countered.

"That isn't possible," Connelly responded. "After the artwork was located, the bunker was sealed up as we found it and no one is aware of its location."

"No one?" Boudreau then said in a sarcastic tone of voice. "We think you might want to rephrase your answer and own up to the truth."

Now getting angry, especially thinking that this was looking more like a set up by Interpol, Connelly told them that no one knew about the bunker or its contents except he and Ms. Marshall.

"Even the German attorney who handled the real estate transaction was not aware of the reason we had chosen that location to purchase property" he said.

"When is the last time you saw Ms. Marshall?" Inspector Bitterman asked.

"It was in New York, right after we returned from Savannah," Connelly replied.

The Inspector then asked her current whereabouts and Connelly said she was in Germany on family business.

"How long has she been in Germany?" Alderman asked.

Connelly explained that she left New York about a month ago to tend to her mother who had become very ill.

Inspector Bitterman then laughed and said "Her mother is dead, Mr. Connelly."

Connelly not quite understanding the Inspectors sarcasm responded "Oh no, that's terrible news."

"It might have been terrible news twenty years ago when it happened, Mr. Connelly, but both of your associate's parents, Ms. Marshall as you call her, died mysteriously in an accident in East Germany. It seems as if he was a member of the Stasi and ran into some difficulty with the KGB in Moscow.

The usually calm, cool and collected Rankin Connelly now was totally unnerved by Bitterman's comment. He wanted to know where Interpol got this information.

Bitterman told him of Interpol's network of affiliates, police agencies around the world where they collect and share information.

"We of course, did background checks on both you and Ms. Marshall when you came under our investigation before you were met by the Chatham County Police Department," he said.

"We didn't want to tip you off about Ms. Marshall in our meeting in Savannah as we wanted to see where this all would lead." he added.

"And where was it that you thought...." Connelly started to say when Bitterman interrupted him.

"Where it would lead........well we knew Ms. Marshall was not who you think she is, her name isn't even Marshall....but Reinhardt," he said to Connelly.

Now fully put off guard by the news of Riva's con, he remarked that a Professor Reinhardt was one of the contacts they found out about when doing research on Amber Room documents.

"Yes, we are aware of those contacts, and we know you never met with Reinhardt," Bitterman said.

Connelly said that she was supposed to meet with Professor Reinhardt when she went back to Germany to tend to her personal affairs. He added that the Professor has written extensively on Hitler and the Nazi's theft of artwork during World War Two.

Bitterman then chuckled again and in a sarcastic tone, "Professor Reinhardt?"

"As far our Interpol contacts in Berlin, there is no Professor Reinhardt, only a Riva Reinhardt with a dead mother and father and no siblings and an Otto Reinhardt who may be her husband," he added.

Shaking his head in disbelief Rankin began to piece together the scenario and began to understand why they suspected his involvement in stolen artwork.

"So you believe Ms. Marshall or Ms. Reinhardt is connected somehow to the stolen artwork which you say has surfaced in the past few months?" Connelly asked.

Boudreau then interjected a question, "Is Ms. Reinhardt still working for you?"

Taking a pause to collect himself, Rankin said that as far as he was concerned that yes, although she was on personal leave, she was still on the Foundation's payroll.

"So for that reason" Alderman said, "you are still a person of interest to Interpol."

Responding, now with contempt in his voice, Connelly said, "Well Interpol might consider me in that way, but I consider Interpol as an organization of interest to me, especially in light of the information you have provided this morning."

Not backing off, Bitterman pressed Connelly for the location of the property and bunker he found on the Austrian-German border.

"I am not at liberty to divulge that information at this point." Connelly responded.

"Let's not get at cross hairs here Mr. Connelly." Bitterman replied. "You need our help and we need your cooperation to get to the bottom of this matter," he added.

Not sure at this point whether he should just move on and ignore the pressure that the Inspector and two agents were bringing to the conversation, or trust his gut and confide in the trio.

The silence in the room was deafening.

Connelly knew the tricks of using long pauses and not responding to questions quickly. He used it very well when bargaining with art collectors over the years.

Finally after looking in each of the eyes of the Interpol agents he said, "In strictest confidence then, the bunker we found is near the border of Germany and Austria. It is located six kilometers outside of Mitterwald on a farm lane off the main road near the train tracks."

Bitterman turned toward Alderman and Boudreau, and interjected that they then will have to involve the German authorities in the plan.

"Involved in what plan?" Connelly asked.

At this point it was Bitterman's long pause that made Connelly somewhat uncomfortable. It felt like the quiet before the storm.

Finally after jotting down notes on the pad sitting in front of him, the Inspector rose to his feet and walked to the sidewall of his office. There he slowly pulled back a sliding cover exposing a blackboard with a pert chart outlining the plan referenced earlier in the conversation.

The Inspector then went on to explain to Connelly the Interpol plan to lure Ms. Marshall to the bunker location with the idea of capturing her and any accomplices she might have….including Professor Reinhardt.

"We want you to arrange with Ms. Marshall, I mean Ms. Reinhardt to meet you at your property. If what you say is true, that you have had no involvement in the artwork recent sales, then Ms. Reinhardt and associates are the prime suspects," Bitterman said.

Now wondering about the involvement of the German police, Connelly asked how they are connected to the operation.

Bitterman explained that Interpol works with the Germans because this is in their territory. "They have a direct interest in the outcome because the artwork you found is in Germany," he added.

Still skeptical about the plan and in some disbelief about the accusations about his associate and love interest Riva Marshall, Connelly asked how Interpol and the Germans planned to have him get her to meet.

That is when Bitterman pulled out the ace of spades and said, "tell her that you have new information on The Amber Room, and believe you have found out where it is located. That should peak her interest and perhaps that of her accomplices."

It was very difficult for Connelly to imagine that a woman who he had spent the last year of his life growing closer physically and emotionally now could be considered someone he would have to lure into a trap.

For Connelly it was more than clearing up his name and reputation with Interpol and the Metropolitan Police in Savannah.

Here in just a half hour discussion with the Inspector and the Interpol agents he saw the unraveling of a wonderful relationship with a beautiful, talented, and most interesting companion. How could Riva Marshall become Riva Reinhardt without him having even a small clue as to the deception? The time for reflection would have to be later he thought. Now is the time to deal with the present and outline how the trap would be set.

Bitterman suggested that Connelly go ahead with his plan to visit the property where the bunker was located. He then added, "but contact Ms. Reinhardt and ask her to meet you tomorrow in the early evening.

"We'll contact you on your cell phone to confirm the plan," Bitterman said. "After you answer, you'll hear a series of three beeps then two beeps and then one. Don't respond, but go to a public telephone and call us on this number," as Bitterman handed a business card to Connelly.

Chapter Fourteen

The Abduction

Following the Interpol meeting Connelly headed back to the Lyon Airport for his two-hour flight to the Munich Airport.

He called Riva from his cell phone on the number she last gave him before she left for Germany. It rings and rings with no answer. He then remembers she called him once, so in checking incoming calls on his cell phone, he finds the number she used.

Again he calls, and finally makes a connection with Riva. He wants very much to ask her about the information given to him by the Interpol agents. Why she lied to him about her name and why she lied about her mother being ill? But he knew if the real story were to be revealed, she wouldn't agree meeting him at the bunker.

After asking about the situation with her mother and masking his knowledge of her betrayal, he asks if she can come to the farm property the next day.

He couldn't help asking also about finding Professor Reinhardt. Her response was less than forthcoming noting that she had some more news about that too, and would tell him about it later.

Following the instructions of Inspector Bitterman, he tells Riva that he too has some very important news to share with her. She asks him not to keep the news from her, but to tell her now. He explains that because of the sensitive nature of the information he can't reveal it on the phone and that she come to the property. He then tells her how much he misses seeing her.

She then agrees to come but not the next day and will take the early morning flight in two days from Berlin to Munich. She says that she must first take care of a few arrangements in Berlin. He agrees and tells her that he will meet her inside the terminal at the visitor's area at 10 a.m.

As he tells Riva goodbye, he hears his flight being announced, so rushes to the gate and boards the plane for his trip to Munich.

After an uneventful flight, he picks up his rental car and heads toward Metterwald. Along the way, he stops for supplies, in case he has to spend more than a few days at the farmhouse. Bitterman's phone call with the plan to trap Riva left him puzzled as to how long he would be at the farmhouse property.

The trip from the airport takes just under two hours and Connelly is tired from all of the activity of the morning. He is constantly thinking of how Riva had fooled him and her duplicity was weighing heavy on his mind.

After arriving at the farmhouse, he gets out of the car and walks toward the farmhouse, pausing momentarily and looks in the direction of the barn where the bunker is located.

He remembers the first day both he and Riva wandered around the property. It seemed as if it was ages ago but in reality was just over a year since unraveling the mysterious map.

He thought of all the experiences he and Riva shared together and was saddened by the knowledge of her faking the feelings of love she so often expressed to him.

Enough of feeling sad and angry he said to himself. His new mission was to understand how artwork he found in the bunker was somehow showing up in various cities in Europe. He knew it wasn't possible unless someone had broken into the bunker.

Once inside the house he begins to pull out a few files from his briefcase and as he begins to review it, the cell phone rings.

He quickly answers the call, listens for the three beep, two beep and one beep code and upon hearing it, turns the phone off and heads out the door.

His instructions were to go immediately to a phone booth in the village. Fortunately in this age of cell phones, Austria still maintained their public phones in small villages.

Once in the village, he looks around cautiously and seeing no one approaches the phone booth. He pulls out the card Inspector Bitterman handed him that morning, and dials the number on the card.

It rings twice and is immediately picked up. The voice on the other end of the line said, "Do we have a confirmation?"

Connelly confirms in the affirmative and notes that Riva agreed to meet him the day after tomorrow at 10 a.m. in the Munich Airport upon her arrival from Berlin. He then asked about the plan referenced earlier.

He is then told not be concerned with the plan, and not to leave the property again until he drives to the airport to meet her. The telephone voice indicates that plainclothes agents will be at the airport terminal waiting for her arrival. The voice then added, "don't worry about the rest of the plan, everything is under control."

Connelly looks around as he hangs the phone up, re-enters his car and drives back to the farmhouse and awaits the trip to the Munich Airport.

His curiosity now aroused, after returning to the farmhouse he makes plans to reenter the bunker. Once inside the barn, he notices that some of the debris covering the old hatch door has been removed. The door is still partially covered, but it is obvious that someone had been there since his last visit.

He then slowly opens the hatch shines his flashlight into the dark bunker and descends down the staircase to the cavernous space beneath the old barn wooden floor.

The beam of the flashlight catches the temporary lighting system that was installed shortly after the bunker's discovery last year. Connelly then flicked the switch and the whole bunker became illuminated.

What he saw then came as a complete surprise. All of the crates that he had carefully stacked up after taking digital photos of each of their contents were not in their original position. Three of them had been opened and the artworks were missing. This might be the explanation of why Interpol thought he had been selling stolen artworks across Europe during the past few months.

So part of the mystery had been solved. But what about Riva, was she the mastermind behind selling the valuable artwork found in the bunker?

Connelly was soon to find out the answer to his question and something else quite unexpected.

Two days later after awakening very early for his drive to the Munich Airport, Connelly parked his rental car and entered the main terminal.

Police dressed as civilians carrying tennis racket covers, which hid their weapons, mingled among the gathering. The airport was busy as travelers were departing and others like him were waiting for arrivals.

Connelly tried to stand by himself some 50 feet or so away from the doors leading from the baggage area. He paced back and forth, as do the plainclothes police awaiting the arrival of Riva. Just before 10:30 a.m. his cell phone rings. He ignores it and then disconnects the call. It rings again after a minute or so. He quickly looks around thinking Riva's plane might have landed late, and he answers the call.

"Hello.....hello....yes can you hear me OK. Where are you....I've been waiting near the arrival area for more than an hour. What? You're where? Outside the terminal in a black Mercedes limo,...but where exactly...okay I'll be right out." Connelly exclaims as he motions to the lead policeman and points to the closest terminal exit.

Holding the cell phone in his hand, he then hurries toward the doors leading to the passenger pick up area and exits the terminal building.

Now standing in a crowd of people, Connelly looks around for a car. A long black Mercedes Limo pulls up and a woman's arm pokes out from the open passenger side front window and motions him to move away from the crowd.

The car moves slowly ahead where no one is standing and the arm beckons him to come closer. As he steps closer to the car, the back door opens; the car then lurches forward and Connelly is knocked to his knees. A man jumps out from the car and pushes Connelly, still grasping his cell phone, inside the back seat as the car speeds away from the terminal.

Connelly is seated in the wide back seat between two people. One is a man in his fifties and the other a tough looking man in his thirties. Riva is in the front while another tough looking man is driving the car. As it speeds out of the airport the car moves onto the highway.

Still groggy from his being knocked down outside the airport, Connelly asks, "What the hell is going on Riva....and who are these people?"

Riva responds, "Rankin I am very sorry, are you OK?"

"OK? Hell no" he responds. "I almost got knocked out, pulled into this car, and.."

Interrupting, Riva said, "I know, I know, again I am sorry your were hurt, but we didn't think you would get in the car willingly."

"Answer my question" Connelly demanded. "What is going on here and what do you mean willingly?"

"It's a long story," Riva responded.

"Ok, give me the short version," Connelly again demanded.

"Well, first of all I'm not who you think I am..." she said.

"What do you mean...... who are you then?" he asked.

"My name isn't important but you can still call me Riva. The rest has to do with the artwork we found in the bunker," she told Connelly.

Yes, I understand, because when I went back there a few days ago...some pieces were missing.

She then said that was part of the story, and the only reason she was telling him anything now, is because of what happened between them.

"I didn't plan on having any feelings for you," Riva added.

Suddenly the man sitting next to Connelly began speaking to Riva in German. He was unaware that Connelly could understand German, not knowing he was once assigned to NATO in Brussels and had to learn both German and French.

The gruff older man, Otto Reinhardt, said, "Cut out the bullshit Riva, and just stick to the plan, I am getting sick of your puppy dog love comments to this asshole here."

Riva now also speaking in German replied, "The plan doesn't mean that I can't be friendly. After all, I spent more than a year with him finding out about the art treasures, it's not like we just met yesterday. Besides we have a long way to go before reaching the destination."

Now grumbling, the man responded, "No, we've changed the destination."

Connelly now interjects, "What's going on now Riva, what are you two talking about?"

Now speaking in English with a heavy German accent the man turns to Connelly and said, "Shut up Mr. Connelly, you're making me nervous, and when I get nervous I sometimes loose my composure."

"God dammit, I demand an explanation of what is going on here," Connelly said.

The man responded to Connelly's question with "Do you understand this?" as he viciously whacks Connelly in the side of the head with the butt of a gun, knocking him out. He then tapes Connelly's mouth shut and binds his wrists together with the tape.

Riva cried out in German, "God damn you Otto, you didn't have to do that."

"Well it will make it easier for you to take care of his final solution when we get to the bunker," he replied.

Marshall then asked if the plan has changed because they were originally going to a warehouse to set up the delivery of the artwork from the bunker.

Otto then told her that there would be no warehouse storage for the artwork, as the new plan was to meet the buyer in Ebersee at the mines.

"First we're going to the Bunker, get the rest of the art work before something else happens. Then Mr. Connelly meets his maker and we leave to meet our buyer," Reinhardt stated.

The drive to the property was uneventful with Connelly out cold in the back next to Reinhardt, and Riva sitting quietly in the front seat.

After speeding to the farmhouse destination, the black limo pulls up to the front of the house. A large moving truck is in the driveway near the barn with a few men standing by its open back doors.

The Limo driver and the other man help Connelly who is still bound, from the car to inside the house.

Reinhardt speaks to the moving truck workers and motions them to follow Riva as she walks toward and into the barn and to the bunker.

Meanwhile inside the farmhouse, Connelly is sitting in a chair still bound but with the gag off his mouth. His head is pounding as a result of the gun butt hit to the side of his head, but he is no longer groggy.

He knows he must get out of the place, before the others return. Only one man is left inside the house guarding him and Connelly needs to get his attention. He speaks to the man who just lit up a cigarette.

"Hey, could you give me a cigarette, I haven't had one since waiting in the airport terminal." Connelly asks.

The man turns around and looks at Connelly with the cigarette still in his mouth and in a strong German accent comments that he thought all Americans got a health message to quit smoking.

"But in your case, it doesn't make any difference if you smoke, since you won't have to worry about cigarettes or anything else once we leave," the man said in a sarcastic tone.

Connelly nods his head, while the tough guy walks over to where Connelly is seated and puts a cigarette in his mouth. Just as he leans over to light it, Connelly head butts him, knocking him backward and to the floor.

Then just as quick, Connelly springs from the chair and with his hands still tied together in front of him, swings both of them together and hits tough man in side of the head just as he is getting up.

This blow knocks him down again. Connelly then lunges at the man, and stomps on his head until the man lays motionless on the floor.

While Connelly and his guard are going at it inside the house, the movers are carrying the now uncrated but wrapped artwork out of the bunker to the waiting truck as the dialogue continues between Reinhardt and Riva.

Speaking in German Reinhardt shouts at the men reminiscent of the same orders given by the Nazi officer 65 years earlier "to keep moving and get the artwork in the truck." He warns the men not to damage anything, and keep the bubble wrapping tight around the art.

He tells Riva to come with him and to take care of Connelly.

"What do you mean take care of him...don't kill him here, it will only lead to me. Do it on the way to the mines," she implores Reinhardt.

"Perhaps you would like to do it 'Ms. Marshall' (laughing derisively) no one will suspect you, since you are his associate, companion and yes, even his lover," he responds.

"You know that the lover part was only to gain access to the artwork. Whatever I did was for you Otto." She said.

"Well that part is all behind us now. I am going to check on Connelly and you finish up here getting everything out and onto the truck." He states.

Connelly has now ripped off the tape, which Reinhardt used to bind his wrists together. The guard still lays motionless on the floor.

Then remembering the trap door discovered during his exploration of the bunker and its various tunnels he pulls the rug back, which covered the trap door.

He runs to the other room and opens the back door and leaves it ajar, then he goes back to the room with the trap door. He quickly lowers himself down a few steps and leans back to pull the rug on the floor so it covers the trap door.

As he disappears into the pitch-black bunker tunnel, Reinhardt enters the now darkened house.

Reinhardt walks quickly over to the man Connelly knocked out, as the man moans and starts to get up.

Reinhardt shakes the guard, who now is standing up and somewhat wobbly.

Yelling in German, Reinhardt said, "Jesus Christ....what the hell happened here....where is Connelly? I said where the fuck is Connelly? Get outside now with the others and find him."

Riva then walks into the house and with a surprised look and begins screaming in German as the man shrugs off being knocked out and stumbles toward the door.

"Where is he?" she shouts at the guard. "You let a bound and gagged man take you out? You fucked up in Savannah and now this? God dammit Otto what kind of fools do you have working for you?"

"Shut up Riva," Reinhardt shouts back. "We have to find that son of a bitch and find him right now and kill him here. Hurry to the car and get the guns out of the trunk."

"Jesus Christ Otto, we'll never find him around here...... it's getting dark outside. Look at the back door... wide open, he probably ran out through the backyard and has gone into the woods," she yells back at Reinhardt.

"Ok, let's get the hell out of here. We'll take care of Connelly later," Reinhardt retorts.

"What do mean later?" Riva asks.

"Later. As in we're going to take the artwork to the Ebensee mine, get a hotel room for the night and then meet our buyer tomorrow. Then we'll come back here, find and kill Connelly. He can't go that far on foot. I knew we should have killed him here and left his body in the bunker. No one would have ever found him." Reinhardt responds.

As Riva and Reinhardt leave the house and drive away in the limo followed closely by the now full moving truck, Rankin is sequestered in the dark bunker.

Using the dimly lit flashlight he quietly makes his way through the tunnel from underneath the farmhouse toward the bunker. He now sees that the end of the tunnel is partially illuminated. The movers in their haste to leave with the artwork failed to turn off the light switch and even left the trap door partially open.

All the artwork is gone and open empty crates are scattered around. He quickly turns off the light thinking that Riva and Reinhardt may come into the barn to see if he somehow escaped to the bunker.

He then makes his way back into the darkened tunnel and disappears from sight.

Chapter Fifteen

The Trap

Inspector Bitterman is sitting at his Interpol Office next to his speakerphone with Alderman and Boudreau standing nearby.

"Any word on Connelly's whereabouts?" he asks the police commander in charge of the Bavarian Landeskriminalamt [LKS] State Police, which does undercover investigations.

The voice on the speakerphone responds, "No, but we have an all points bulletin out for his whereabouts."

Bitterman with an edge to his voice asks what happened at the airport and why the plainclothes police stationed there didn't see what happened to Connelly when he left the airport.

Responding to Bitterman's questions, the commander on the speakerphone gave an overview of the situation from the time the police arrived at their appointed positions and when they lost sight of Connelly.

He said that they were in the terminal as planned well before 10 a.m. waiting with Connelly for Ms. Reinhardt's arrival. By 10:30 they were getting anxious that perhaps she had somehow changed her arrival plans. He said they noticed Connelly begin speaking on his cell phone and then quickly left the visitors area to the terminal exit.

Our men also moved quickly, trying not to alarm anyone standing in that part of the terminal. As soon as they reached the outside they encountered a crowd of people waiting near the curbside pick up area. At that point they spotted Connelly being put into a black Mercedes limo, which sped away." he said.

Then the voice on the speaker phone added, "By the time our men got into their cars, they lost sight of the limo and airport traffic blocked any chance of catching up to it."

"So no car ID, and license number?" Bitterman asks.

"Well, airport cameras did catch the license plate of the Mercedes; and we traced the car to one Otto Reinhardt whose address is in Berlin." he responded.

He then added, "Our intra city patrols were alerted immediately to be on the look out, but you must know how many black Mercedes there are on German roads."

Bitterman then asks if any of his men checked the area near Mitterwald to see if it was possible that Connelly somehow was taken there.

The commander said that after exploring other possibilities, they went to the area near Mitterwald where Connelly had purchased property the year before based upon the information given to them by Interpol. They looked inside the farmhouse and found nothing out of the ordinary, except some tape and Connelly's briefcase and overnight bag.

Bitterman's second phone line begins to ring and he ignores it momentarily. It continues to ring and after a minute tells the commander he will call him right back.

He then answers the second line.

"Hello.....yes...yes I can hear you...Jesus...where are you....and are you alright?" Bitterman inquires.

He then turns on his speakerphone for Alderman and Boudreau to listen in on the conversation.

Connelly tells them that he is okay considering he was kidnapped in front of the German police at the Munich Airport and then roughed up and knocked out by Riva's henchmen.

"So, where are you now?" the Inspector asks Connelly.

"At the village at the public phone booth," he responds.

Bitterman tells him that the German Police said they were at the farmhouse last night looking for him.

"They went in the house and found your briefcase and a few personal belongings, but no sight of you," he explained.

"Oh my God," Connelly replies. "I heard people in the house, but I thought Reinhardt and his henchmen had come back looking for me."

"So where were you when the police came looking for you?" Bitterman asks.

Connelly then tells him about his escape through the tunnel under the farmhouse. He said that he was bound and gagged shortly after leaving the airport, and that in addition to Riva; there were Reinhardt and two thugs in the limo.

They drove directly to Mitterwald from the Munich Airport stopping only to pick up lunch. They then spent time taking the artwork out of the crates, repacking it in special plastic wrapping and putting it into a moving truck.

Connelly asks if the Mercedes has been located yet.

"No, not yet...but we have a solid lead," the Inspector replies.

"Do you have GPS tracking for cell phones at Interpol?" Connelly asks.

"What do you mean?" Bitterman said.

"When I got the phone call from Riva at the airport I didn't turn it off in my rushing to go outside and find her. And when I was knocked down, I still had it in my hand, so after being shoved into the car I pushed my cell phone in between the back of the seat and the seat itself before I was knocked out." Connelly said.

"God that's good work Connelly and yes we can have the German and Austrian Police track it...and I'll do it immediately," Bitterman exclaims.

"Ok, I will wait to hear from you," Connelly responds.

He is then told to return to the farmhouse and not to leave under any circumstances and that the Austrian National Police will pick him up in a few hours.

Later that morning, an Austrian police helicopter lands in front of the farmhouse. Connelly hears it and rushes outside to greet the police officers. After brief introductions, the trio get into the chopper and it flies away.

Connelly is pleasantly surprised how good the two officers speak in English, and asks about their destination.

He is told that the GPS tracking system showed the cell phone location and that the Mercedes is currently outside the Austrian village of Ebensee.

"That name jumps out right at me," Connelly said. It was the location of the last concentration camp of the Nazi's and was liberated by U.S. Troops in May 1945.

The pilot responds, "Yes, it has a dark cloud hanging over it from those days. It still has salt mines however, but many others have been abandoned. The car was tracked to one of these abandoned salt mines outside of the village."

Ranking asks how long it will take them to get there and was told depending on wind conditions it might take an hour or less.

He then comments about how convenient for Reinhardt and his henchmen to find a place to store the artwork by taking a page out of the Nazi playbook.

The police officer looking puzzled turns to Rankin and said "Nazi playbook?"

"Yes.....the Nazis stored a lot of their stolen art in salt mines in this area, but it was found by the U.S. Army after the war," Connelly said.

The helicopter flies over what Rankin sees as the most beautiful parts of Austria. Even though he was there last year meeting with Steinbacker in Vienna Barlinger in Linz, and D'Alivia in Salzburg, the view from the helicopter flying high above the landscape of mountains, lakes and valleys was breathtaking.

After less than an hour, the helicopter lands outside the perimeter of a line of policemen who have erected barricades to keep onlookers away from the scene.

Rankin is quickly escorted to the command vehicle location and introduced to the field commander. He is told that he must stay back away from the entrance, as it could be very dangerous if the suspects do not surrender peacefully.

Rankin seeing that the black Mercedes is a short distance away from the entrance parked behind the large moving truck, makes his way toward it in an attempt to retrieve his cell phone.

Just as the commander finishes his warning, gunshots ring out from the mouth of the mine entrance, as Connelly retrieves the cell phone from the back seat. He quickly ducks down.

The police are ordered to hold their fire....as one of the police closest to Connelly, begins speaking on a megaphone.

"Attention. Attention." The commander's voice rings out over the loud speaker. "Otto Reinhardt, we know you are in the mine. We ask that you come out peacefully. We do not want to hurt you, but just come out to speak with us. You will not be harmed."

There is no response from the mine entrance.

Rankin then thinks he might be able to reach Riva inside the mine. He motions to the commander to have him try reaching Riva with his cell phone.

The commander yells to Connelly, "I doubt if it will work there can't be any mobile service in there.....but give it a try....just ask that they come out with their hands held high....and no weapons."

Rankin dials his cell phone and waits for a response and shouts into his phone, "Riva please answer." But the cell phone continues to ring and ring with no contact.

Rankin puts the cell phone in his pocket and walks dejectedly away from the group of policemen.

All of a sudden there is a volley of gunfire emanating from the mine's entrance...policemen scatter and return the gunfire, cars are hit.

Suddenly an explosion is heard coming from inside the mine, then more explosions, and part of the hill begins to cave in on the entrance of the mine. Then silence as the dust plume rises against the pale blue sky.

The Commander motions to Rankin to move back saying there could be more explosions, as the mine may have had explosives hidden away in one of the side tunnels.

Rankin yells, "Is there another way out of there?"

"Maybe, most of these mines had an emergency exit" the commander yells back. "Perhaps it's over there on the side of the hill. Let me find out what if anything is happening there."

The police commander opens his cell phone and dials a number...he waits impatiently for a number of seconds then begins speaking.

"Do you see anything at that end......yes we saw explosions here....what?.....someone is coming out of the emergency exit.....stop him and we'll be right there....any other survivors? None that you see, Ok just hold the suspect but don't harm him. Got it"

"Man?" Rankin asks.

"Man." Replies the commander.   "Let's go."

Connelly follows the police commander and a few of his men as they run around to the side of the hill toward the smoke which is drifting out of an opening.....a man covered in soot is on the ground...being handcuffed by a policeman.

The suspect is helped to his feet with his back to Connelly but then turns around shaking as he spots Rankin

"My God it can't be, what is he doing here?" Rankin exclaimed.

"What? You know this man?" The commander asks Connelly. "Is it Reinhardt?"

"No not Reinhardt, but yes I know him. His name is Robert Vestry." Rankin said.

Still not quite believing his eyes he exclaimed to no one in particular, "What the fuck?"

Vestry with his head hanging down, his face not quite visible as it is covered with soot faces Rankin. His back is to the tunnel still spewing forth smoke and dust.

Ranking goes closer to the now shackled Vestry and asks, "What the hell are you doing here, and how are you connected to these thugs?"

"It's a long story Rankin.....and one that wasn't suppose to end this way," he responds.

The Police Commander then pulls Vestry away and said "You're right about that, and your story doesn't end here either. Come on, let's go."

Rankin asks the Police Commander to wait and give him just a few minutes with the suspect. He responds with a nod of his head as other police gather around.

"We didn't want any violence," Vestry said. "I just wanted the artwork and knew you wouldn't part with it, at least not the way we wanted.

"But why?" Rankin asks. "I don't understand. What the hell were you thinking?"

"I am so very sorry Rankin. I thought that this would be an easy transaction...no one was to get hurt. You know that I am a major art collector and desperately wanted these hidden treasures." Vestry responded.

"Now of course no one will have them because the artwork you found in that Nazi bunker is buried here forever," as Vestry points to the smoldering tunnel entrance.

"Not quite," Rankin replies. "You see if you were going to buy these works of art [pointing toward the now caved in hill side] you were going to be buying the copies I had made in China."

149

He then told Vestry that the plan to steal the artwork was all in vain because the artworks Reinhardt took from the bunker the day before were fakes.

Vestry in disbelief asked again about the artwork now covered in the exploded mine.

"What? That's unbelievable. Reinhardt told me he had those works checked out...and all had impeccable provenance," he exclaimed.

Rankin then told him, "The originals are still here in Austria....safely stored in a climate controlled facility, awaiting identification from the potential heirs of the owners."

"I had my suspicions about something possibly happening to the bunker treasures after returning with the artwork copies from China," Connelly said.

"My concern was someone might uncover the location of the bunker so when the opportunity presented itself I placed the copies in the bunker and moved the originals to safe keeping," he added.

"My God what a fool I have been......" Vestry replied.

Rankin said, as he turned away, "I would never have guessed that you of all people would betray not only me but the memory of my father, your life long friend."

At this point the Police Commander asked Rankin who the suspect is and how he knows him.

"This is the attorney who handled my father's estate; who handled many of the legal affairs of the

Connelly Art Foundation; who has been an advisor to me during this past year since my father's death. This is Robert Vestry III," Connelly replied with disdain.

"He was the one who introduced me to Riva Marshall, I mean Reinhardt, who is now buried under all that rubble," Connelly pointing toward the tunnel.

"Wait, no you're wrong," Vestry said. "Riva and Otto had a falling out last night at the hotel, and he left her there this morning. She said she was through with him, and I think she left for the train station."

Rankin with a stunned look on his face said, "My God, I thought she had to be dead from the explosion."

"Come on," the Commander said, motioning to one of his assistants to take Vestry toward the waiting vehicles. "We'll finish this at headquarters.....I'm sure Interpol would like to complete the story."

As the Commander and the police begin walking away Rankin is left standing alone looking back wistfully at the tunnels emergency exit still in shock thinking about what had just transpired.

The Commander turns abruptly around and yells out to Connelly, "And oh, Mr. Connelly, you can expect a call from Inspector Bitterman. He wants to discuss something about Amber Room documents, and offer his....uh....personal apologies on behalf of Interpol."

Just then Rankin's cell phone rings and he thinks that yes, he is due a major apology from the Inspector.

"Hello Inspector…..hello……hello…..can you hear me?" he shouts. But then he hears a woman's voice on the other end of the line.

"Oh my God, Riva is that you? Yes I can hear you," he says in an excited voice.

Then suddenly his cell phone goes dead after being hidden in the limo since the day before.

Connelly shakes his head, looks at his cell phone and thinks "one mystery solved and another begins."

The search for The Amber Room continues.

ABOUT THE AUTHOR

djv murphy [Dennis J. Murphy] received his elementary and secondary education at St. Michaels Parochial School in Flint, Michigan. He received an undergraduate degree in communications from Michigan State University and an M.B.A. from the University of Miami.

As an executive with non profit organizations for many years, his career took him from coast to coast [Ohio, California, New York, Virginia, Connecticut, and New Jersey]. In the mid 1990's his interest in fine arts led him to open a highly successful gallery in the small town of High Bridge, New Jersey. *"galleryONEmain"* exhibited the works of more than 200 artists from countries around the world.

He currently owns the internet based art site, *carpediemartgallery.com* and manages investment properties in New Jersey and Georgia. He has won awards for his renovations of historic buildings as well as awards for his writing.

His most recent published works include the award winning screenplays "Amber Room Treasures", "You Can Call Me Jay", Abduction at Dawn"; and books, "Life, Love, Remembrances", "So You Want To Become A Landlord....Tales From the Crypt", and "Letters From Mother". All may be found on the website *bunkertreasures.com* and on *Amazon.com*

Murphy is the father of four children; Dr. John Murphy and Dr. Denise Stadelmaier of Midland, Michigan; Jerry Murphy of Chatham, NJ; and currently resides on Carpe Diem Farm in Central

New Jersey with his daughter Mariden and German Shepherd dog "Boston".

CPSIA information can be obtained at www.ICGtesting.com
Printed in the USA
BVOW05s2232050415

394844BV00001B/32/P